"Laura, I have two favors to ask of you."

Seth went on, "I'm sorry, but I have to ask."

"What?" Favors? What exactly could she do for him?

"If we run into the men, I'm going to fight them as best as I can. I need you to take Abby and run, okay? Through the river or wherever you think is the safest. But let me fight and distract them and buy you some time. Please?"

That was a favor for him? It seemed like a favor for her. But Laura knew why he was asking. The thought of leaving Seth to near certain death hit her harder than she would have ever imagined. He was a park ranger. A stranger.

And she did not want him to die.

"Okay. I'll try, Seth." She hoped that was good enough.

"The second favor is a bigger one. When you get out of this, I want you to get a message to my family. Will you please tell them that I'm sorry and that I love them?"

Victoria Austin lives in the American Midwest with her husband, children and dogs. Her kids write notes in the furniture dust and the family watches television with the closed captioning on because the house is, um, loud. She likes chocolate, peace and quiet, chocolate and silence. She gets too much of one and too little of the other. This explains the tight pants and the many, many, many gray hairs.

Books by Victoria Austin

Love Inspired Suspense

Rocky Mountain Showdown

Love Inspired Historical

Family of Convenience

Visit the Author Profile page at Harlequin.com for more titles.

ROCKY MOUNTAIN SHOWDOWN

VICTORIA AUSTIN

HARLEQUIN® LOVE INSPIRED® SUSPENSE

LOVE INSPIRED BOOKS

Recycling programs for this product may not exist in your area.

ISBN-13: 978-1-335-67880-5

Rocky Mountain Showdown

Fear not; for thou shalt not be ashamed: neither be thou confounded; for thou shalt not be put to shame: for thou shalt forget the shame of thy youth, and shalt not remember the reproach of thy widowhood any more.

–*Isaiah* 54:4

To my family–

I have everything because I have you.

ONE

The first thing Laura Donovan saw when she regained consciousness was the man leaning over her.

The first thing she felt was her fist connecting with his jaw.

"Hey!" the man exclaimed, stepping back quickly while holding his jaw. His hat fell to the floor.

Laura scrambled to her feet, trying to keep an eye on the man while desperately scanning the cabin for Abby. She didn't see her daughter anywhere. "Where's my daughter?" Laura was breathing hard like she had just run for miles, and she could feel her heart pounding in her chest. The muscles in her fingers tightened as she thought about fighting this man. She would do it if she had to. She would do anything to save her daughter.

The man's eyes widened and his hand moved

away from his face. Instead, he held both hands in front of him, palms out, as if trying to show Laura that he was harmless. He was looking at Laura like she was a crazy person. "Your daughter?"

The man was dressed like a park ranger, right down to the ridiculous hat. Maybe he was a park ranger, since Mahoney's men had all been dressed in black from head to toe. Laura didn't care. She did not have time for this game. She had no idea how long she'd been unconscious, and she had no idea where Mahoney and his men were.

"Abby! Abigail!" Laura tried to sound calm, but there was no keeping the emotion from her voice. "It's okay, honey! Please come out. Please!" Laura ran into the cabin's first bedroom, flung open the closet door and dropped to her belly to look under the bed. Nothing. She ran into the bathroom and frantically pulled open the cupboard doors looking for the three-year-old. Where was she?

Please let her be hiding. Please let her be in the cabin. Please, please, please. Abby had to be terrified. What if she had run outside? What if Mahoney took her? What if he didn't, instead just killing the girl? Her baby.

No.

"It's okay, Abby! Mommy promises. Please

come out." Laura ran to the closet in the second bedroom and threw the door open. She fell to her knees, crying in relief. Abby was there on the closet floor, arms locked around her knees pulling them tightly into her chest. She just looked at her mother, tears running down her cheeks.

"Abby. Oh, Abby. Come here, baby. It's okay, just come here." Laura pulled her sweet girl into her arms, then stood up while trying to press the child's warmth as close to her body as possible. Laura turned and swallowed hard when she saw the park ranger standing in the doorway.

He still had his hands held out in front of him, still had a confused look on his face.

Laura froze, trying to decide what to do. She had Abigail. Her daughter was okay. She was okay.

"Mrs. Donovan?" The ranger's voice was soft like he was trying to calm a wild animal.

Laura felt a whole lot like a wild animal right now.

"Get out of my way. Now." She sounded deranged, and that was not far from the truth. Laura needed to get her daughter out of the cabin. Off the mountain. And that man was standing between them and the door. His weapon was still holstered, and Laura decided he probably was a park ranger. One who had picked today to come check out the recluse living on the mountain.

"I don't know what I walked into, Mrs. Donovan. But I'm not the enemy here."

Laura's short laugh was bitter. Sure he wasn't. Even before this terrible, terrible day, park rangers had never been her friend. Laura couldn't tell if she was shaking or if the vibrations were from Abby, but either way they were less than stable. She needed to get it together.

Laura wished she could wipe her sweaty hands off on her jeans. Relax her shaky arms. Find some medicine for her pounding headache. But that would mean letting go of Abby and that wasn't happening. She sucked in a breath, trying to make the flow slow and steady. And subtle. The bright lights that had been floating in her vision faded. The haze of static in her head cleared.

"How do you know my name?" She sounded like she was accusing him of something. Because she kind of was.

"I told you. I'm a park ranger assigned to this part of Colorado. I know most of the people who live bordering the public lands."

"Great. You're not the enemy. Congratulations. Get out of my way." Laura tried to sound as authoritative as possible.

The ranger took a step back but Laura did not move forward. He didn't look like any of Mahoney's men, and that uniform looked authentic, but Laura wasn't sure what was real anymore. Not after today. He was still too close for her comfort.

"Mrs. Donovan, I don't know what is going on. But I can help you. My name is Seth."

Laura snorted. "You think you can help, huh? Just wandered up here on the off chance I needed some help?"

His eyes were still wary and confused. "Yes. There's a fire out there. I got caught up in it while doing patrol. The only way out was up the mountain toward your land. I passed your cabin on my way and stopped to warn you. That's when I found you."

Laura bit her lip for a second. Okay. That rang true. And, more important, his vehicle sounded like a way to get off the mountain. Mahoney had slashed her tires earlier. Right in front of her. Just to show her how completely trapped she really was. "All right. Let's go." She jerked her chin, indicating that he should walk in front of her and she would follow.

Seth looked unsure. "Yeah. We'll go. But

what did I walk in on? Why were you unconscious on the floor? Are you okay? I mean, what's going on?"

Laura swallowed, increasing the pressure of her arms around Abby even though she had already been holding the girl tightly. "It doesn't matter. We need to get out of here."

Bringing his hand back to his face, he rubbed the place where she had hit him and looked at Abby. Then he nodded and turned to walk through the living room and out the cabin door.

Laura took a deep breath and kissed Abby on the top of her head. "Okay, honey. Okay. We're going to go away from this now. It will be all right." Abby just pushed farther into Laura's front in response.

Seth had walked out. Laura needed to follow.

She exited the cabin's front door and saw a park ranger's truck parked in front. Seth really was a ranger. Once Laura was off this mountain, she would appreciate the irony of a ranger saving Malcolm Grant's daughter.

Seth was standing by the passenger side of the truck, holding the door open and waiting for her. She was a couple yards away, walking quickly, when the gunshot came from her left. Out of the forest. Seth was to her before she realized he'd moved. He grabbed her and began to pull. Away from the gunshot. Before Laura fully comprehended what was going on, she and Seth were back inside the cabin, and he slammed the front door shut.

"I only heard the one shot, but that doesn't mean there's only one shooter."

Seth didn't sound nearly as shaky as Laura felt. He had walked over to one of the windows and was peeking through the curtains with a gun in his hand. She hadn't seen him take it out. Belatedly, stupidly, Laura realized she was just standing there holding Abigail.

Reaching for an empty loop on his pants, Seth patted around his belt with a force that matched the intensity coming off him as he looked down. He let out a deep huff. Before Laura's brain could catch up with her runaway nerves, he was focusing all that intensity on her. "My radio must have fallen off when I ran. Please tell me you have one. I radioed in about the fire before I got here, but I need to call in for help with a shooter."

Laura was shaking her head before Seth even finished the question. "No. We don't get cell service this far up the mountain, and we don't have a radio."

"What about for emergencies? If you or Abby needed help?"

Laura's mouth tightened. "We rely on ourselves up here on the mountain. We don't like outsiders."

Laura watched his face, her stomach tightening. She knew the rumors surrounding her father. People said Malcolm Grant was the stereotypical ex-soldier turned recluse. Antisocial. Living off the grid and holding himself accountable to no law or authority. They were wrong, of course. But Laura had given up defending her father to people like park rangers long ago.

The man quickly moved back to the window, peering through the curtains. He spoke to her without looking her way, his voice curt but not entirely mean. "I think now is a good time for you to tell me what in the world is going on." He was moving as he talked, pushing the couch in front of the door.

The ranger moved through the living room, pushing the table against the back door. The cabin was really only four rooms—the living area/kitchen, two bedrooms and the bathroom. Now that both outside doors were blocked, Seth was looking out the windows again.

Laura didn't know where to start. Or what to say. "There is a man named Victor Mahoney. He is trying to kill me."

"Why?"

"I don't know."

Seth looked ready to argue with her when a second shot sounded. Laura heard it hit the outside of the cabin. She thought she could feel the walls shake from the impact, even though she knew that had to be her mind playing tricks on her.

Seth's face turned grim. "We need to get out of here."

How had all this happened? Laura didn't know. But she was trapped in the cabin with a park ranger. And Mahoney was outside still trying to kill them.

So now she was relying on the park ranger for help. He'd saved them. Maybe. Park rangers were always the enemy. Twenty years of being her father's daughter had taught her that. She'd watched park rangers harass, and even arrest on occasion, her father more times than she could remember. Her father refused to follow their rules. He wasn't hurting anyone, but the rangers couldn't let it go.

But, when faced with Victor Mahoney, this

particular one was probably the lesser of two threats. Maybe.

Help us, Lord.

Laura had closed her eyes as she prayed. Habit. When she opened them, the ranger had this look on his face. An almost gentle expression, though the gentleness was offset by the tight lines around his mouth. As quickly as it had appeared though, it was gone. He went to check the other window again.

Laura's head hurt. She missed her dad. He would know what to do. From the day he'd adopted her, he had known what to do. She looked at the cabin door and could hear her dad's gravelly voice in her head. So rough and blunt, but never cutting. *"Get it together, girl. Be still. Assess. Plan. Try."*

"Okay, Ranger, let's make some plans." When she spoke, the ranger turned from where he had been peering out the window.

"Seth."

Laura was jolted from her imposed calm. Disjointed again. "Seth?"

His smile was slight and his voice did not betray the urgency of the situation. "I told you, my name is Seth. Seth Callahan. Maybe you can say it without the venom you use with the word *ranger.*"

The smile was absorbed by hard lines again as a third shot came in through the window, sending glass flying everywhere.

Yep, he had definitely walked into something. Something bad. His routine patrol had turned into an unexpected fire had turned into a detour onto Old Man Grant's property. Seth had suspected that he might receive a hostile welcome when he walked up to the cabin door, but this was beyond hostile. This felt like a siege.

Once Seth ventured another look out the now-broken window, he could see at least two men out there. They were dressed in black, wearing dark sunglasses, and had earbuds. This wasn't good. Seth didn't need to rely on his military training to recognize an assault team when he saw one, though it certainly helped to solidify the feeling of dread in his stomach.

At least they hadn't fired a second shot into the cabin. Yet, anyway.

The doors were blocked. For now. But a couple pieces of furniture were not going to keep those men out for long. They needed a plan. And some serious help. *Please, God. Show me what to do. Give me the strength to do it.* That prayer had almost become a daily plea when Seth had been in Afghanistan. And an hourly one when he was in the hospital and rehab center. And now it was back, seemingly his default mode when his life fell apart.

Seth took a deep breath, trying to be as calm as possible around Laura. Whatever this was, she was clearly hurt and upset. And, well, she should be, given their current predicament. He had left this morning for what was supposed to be a simple patrol, not a foray into an action movie. Seth had put combat behind him. Now, it seemed, it was back in his life.

Seth looked back out the window. The men were holding their position. For now. They were not firing their weapons. For now.

Laura was still clutching her daughter, who seemed to have snuggled up on Laura's chest. Seth just stared. It was rude and this was definitely not the time, but he couldn't help himself. The child looked…well, little. Seth tried to remember what his nieces had looked like before he left his hometown. The girl in Laura's arms seemed about the same age Beth had been when he last saw her. That would make her around three years old. Beth wasn't three anymore. And he had missed it.

Laura murmured something else to the girl,

though Seth couldn't make it out. The tone was comforting and reassuring. She looked at him, indicating the girl with her chin. "This is my daughter. Abigail. Abby."

Seth moved from the window, trying not to be offended by the way Laura tightened her hold on Abby and shifted away from him as he approached. He walked past Laura and Abby to see what the situation was in the bedrooms. There was a window in each one, but no door. Looking out the bedroom window, he tried to make his voice low and calm. But he wanted to keep Laura informed.

Plus, he needed her. The public, including rangers, had not been welcome up here for decades. Old Man Grant excelled at keeping people off his land. Laura knew this mountain, and she knew what resources they had available inside the cabin. They were going to need her expertise to get out of this.

"I don't see anyone else—just the two men out front. How many men did this Mahoney guy have with him?"

Laura's dark eyes were serious and she kept one hand moving in a steady circle on Abby's back. "Eight maybe? I was more focused on him and the gun he had pointed at Abby."

"Why are they trying to kill you?" He

looked at Abby, not wanting to frighten her. But he had to know, and the situation was beyond urgent. "Why did they leave you unconscious on the floor only to try to shoot you later?"

Laura's voice was a sound of anguish. "I gave them what they wanted. I gave them the key. Then he said he wanted our deaths to look like an accident. He hit me. I don't know how this happened."

What key was she talking about? Every instinct Seth had was screaming at him to quit talking and start acting. But he'd seen more than one mission go sideways because of bad information. Getting the details correct was often the difference between life and death. "I need you to back up. Start at the beginning."

"I found a safe-deposit key last week. This Mahoney came up the mountain today. With a lot of armed men. He said he wouldn't hurt us if we gave him the key."

"But he lied."

Laura actually rolled her eyes at him. "Clearly." Her voice was dry. Sarcastic.

"What's in the safe-deposit box?"

"I don't know," she said.

"How do you not know?" This was not the time for Laura to keep details to herself.

"I didn't even know the box existed. My husband, Josh, was killed eighteen months ago. I just boxed all his stuff up when we came back here. Last week was the first time I opened them. That's when I found it."

Seth had heard that Old Man Grant's daughter had moved back home. She'd stayed even after Grant had died.

Seth quickly walked to the front windows and tried to look out without being seen. The two men were still there, not moving or talking. Assault teams were very good at waiting. He made his way to the windows in the back of the cabin. Nothing but typical Colorado mountain terrain. Two men out front in plain sight. Nothing visible anywhere else. Seth's clenched stomach tightened even further. Those men had a plan and Seth knew he wasn't going to like it.

"Laura, we still need a plan. If we can't call for assistance, then we have to figure out some other way of getting it. Some other way to communicate that we are in trouble. We need help. Backup. More people with guns on our side."

Laura held her daughter closer to her body and shrugged her shoulders in an almost desperate manner. "I don't have any way to call for help. Believe me, if I did, I would have used it when the shooting started."

Seth blew out an angry breath. He hated this feeling. This trapped and useless sinkhole that he somehow found himself back in. His voice was harsh, but getting shot by the two men out front would definitely be harsher. "Well, think. You said you gave them what they wanted? So they just left? Then why are they back?"

Seth sounded accusatory. Too bad. It needed to be asked and being nice was going to get them killed if they didn't figure out how to get out of this situation.

Laura's voice was almost stiff. "They knew I had the key to the safe-deposit box. They said if I gave it to them, they would leave. I did." Her voice became even more brittle. "They lied. They said they had to kill us but it needed to look like an accident."

The fire. It had to be the fire. Seth had been completely surprised at the fire when he came across it while out patrolling. He'd assumed it was started by careless campers. Now he knew.

Laura wasn't done. "They said the smoke from the fire would kill me and Abby long before the actual flames. I panicked. They hit me, and the next thing I knew was you were there waking me up."

Seth exhaled deeply. He had asked and now he knew. The men must have been watching from somewhere safe to make sure the fire actually consumed the cabin. The cabin with an unconscious woman and a three-year-old little girl inside.

Seth looked out the window again. The men were still waiting. The more the men outside stayed still, the more Seth felt like he needed to be doing something. Standing and waiting for someone else to act did not sit well with him. He wouldn't—no he couldn't—play the victim and wait to see what his fate would be.

He wondered if something had gone wrong with the fire. While it was certainly healthy when he'd come across it, it wasn't moving terribly fast. It had run horizontally, blocking the road back down. And it would eventually reach the cabin and probably burn it down. But it wasn't going to do so in the next few hours.

This Mahoney must have started the fire far away from the cabin so it wouldn't look deliberate. But he'd miscalculated. And now it seemed that Mahoney would settle for Laura and Abby dying even if it didn't look accidental.

Seth really wanted to know more about this Mahoney and how Laura found herself in this situation. But not now—right now, Seth wanted a satellite phone and an extraction team. He wasn't going to get either. He needed to be smart and deliberate. And quick. He doubted the men would wait much longer.

Laura was just looking at him. Her hand was still making that steady circle on Abby's back. Her other arm must be hurting from supporting all of Abby's weight, but Laura wasn't showing any signs of stopping. The little girl was resting her head on her mother's shoulder, breathing into Laura's neck. One tiny fist clutched a stuffed yellow duck. She looked warm and sleepy. Safe. Seth glanced at the back door. The clear path into the forest. They could make a run for it, but it wouldn't work.

Laura spoke, her eyes also on the back door. "We won't make it, will we?" It wasn't really a question. Seth wanted to puff out his chest, flex his muscles and tell her that he would keep her and her daughter safe. That he could pick them both up and run them out that back door. Run them to safety. But Laura deserved honesty more than false assurances.

"No. If there are two men out front, then someone has to be watching the back. Even if they aren't, the men out front would hear us. Chase us. And we—"

Laura finished for him. "Have Abby. We're trapped."

TWO

Trapped. They were trapped. Inside a cabin, surrounded by men with guns. Men who had been very clear about wanting to kill both Laura and sweet Abigail.

And Laura didn't even know what this was all about. Why?

Laura hugged Abby more closely to her body, breathing in the smell of children's shampoo, grilled cheese and that musky scent that came from playing in the forest. Abby's body was warm and slightly damp from when Laura had piled blankets on top of her and put her down for her nap. The fever she'd been fighting all week was gone for now.

One little foot was bare. Laura found her other shoe and put it on, feeling better that Abby was fully dressed. She ran her hands over the small feet, then went back to rubbing a circle on Abby's back, though that was more for her own benefit than the little girl's. Abby was asleep, but the repetition and physical contact soothed Laura. Grounded her. Reminded her that she and Abby were here together. Abby was the only thing Laura needed in this world.

Laura wanted to go look out the window for herself, but she made her legs stay where they were. She wasn't sure she would be able to peer through the curtains without being detected. And those men had already shown they were willing to shoot in.

She didn't want to put Abby down, and she sure didn't want to carry Abby closer to the window—to the men with guns. Laura wished again that her dad were still here. He would know what to do. How to make it right.

Laura smiled as she thought of what he'd say. His voice would be exasperated. Never out of patience with her, but his tone would have suggested that the answer was right there in front of her. Obvious and logical. *"Use the tunnel, girl. It's an escape tunnel. Escape in it."*

The tunnel. Laura sucked in a deep breath, her hand faltering in its circle pattern. How could she have forgotten? When she had first come to live with her dad, she'd been convinced he was some sort of alien. He lived on a mountain. A whole mountain to himself. He talked about not going into *their world*. And he had a tunnel. It made sense to a seven-year-old.

Laura had found it by accident about a month after coming to the mountain. She had refused to go hunting with Malcolm Grant, still stuck in the grief of losing her parents and the surreal timidity that came with finding herself living on a strange mountain with a new dad.

Mad at herself for crying, yet again, she had thrown her stuffed teddy bear as hard as she could. He'd landed in the closet. After a few minutes of telling herself she wasn't a baby and didn't need the silly bear, Laura had climbed off the bed and retrieved her only friend. And she had discovered the latch to the tunnel.

Laura smiled, remembering that moment so clearly. She had lifted the trapdoor, found a flashlight and jumped into the tunnel without thinking. Laura didn't know enough to be afraid. All Laura knew was that aliens were real, and she was going to take that tunnel to a different planet. She'd talked out loud as she explored, encouraging the aliens to come out and play. They never did, of course.

Her dad had been livid when he found her several hours later. It was the closest he'd ever come to yelling at her. "It's an escape tunnel, girl. Not a playground. It's secret. And we both need to pray to God that we'll never, ever need to use it."

And they hadn't. Until now.

Laura tried to take a deep breath, hoping it would calm her. *Please, God, let this be the right decision.* "I know how we can get out. There's a tunnel."

"A tunnel." Seth sounded like he had just been told that there was a teleportation device hidden in the cabin. Laura couldn't blame him.

"Yes, a tunnel. An escape tunnel. My dad made it, when he built the cabin. For situations like this." Laura's voice didn't betray the absurdity of those words. Incredulity might be an expected response to a secret escape tunnel, but Laura was loyal to her dad. Even though he'd been dead for a few months now, she was never going to betray him by mocking him. Especially not in front of park rangers.

"Your dad often find himself being shot at by random people?"

Laura tried to hide her wince. She had spent most of her life hearing people criticize her dad, and she had learned to ignore them. Kind of.

"I'm sorry, Laura. I shouldn't—"

"Stop." Her voice was loud. Loud and tired and just a touch desperate.

Her little girl moved at the sound of Laura's voice, lifting her head and opening her eyes. Laura straightened her back, holding Abby more firmly to her chest. She placed her hand on the back of the child's head, pushed it back into the indent of her neck and breathed in deeply, her nose still in the child's hair.

She didn't have time for this, and she had more important things to do right now than defend her dad to this park ranger. Her eyes never broke contact with Seth. Her voice was softer. She didn't feel like forgiving him or being kind to him. She just felt...weary. Laura suddenly felt very, very weary.

"Just stop. You said we have to get out of here quickly. I'm telling you there's a way out. I'm going to take it. Are you coming with me?"

Before Seth could open his mouth to answer, Laura was moving again. She meant it about taking the tunnel out of here. Laura wasn't crazy about going alone, but she would if he didn't follow. She headed back to the small bedroom and opened the closet door. She got down on her knees, setting Abby on the floor.

"Here, honey, sit here for Mommy for just a second. Okay?" Laura took a moment to rub her hand over the sleepy girl's cheek. She nodded and leaned against the wall. Satisfied, Laura turned once again to the open closet.

Laura somehow found a latch in the floor— the trapdoor into a tunnel. Standing, she then reached up to the top shelf of her closet and pulled out a couple flashlights. She handed one to Seth, who was standing close to her, just watching.

Then she opened the trapdoor and saw the ladder leading down into the dark. Cool air drifted up, along with the scent of damp earth. Laura didn't remember the tunnel feeling like a grave when she'd been a child. It did now, though.

The goose bumps that broke out on Laura's arm had nothing to do with the temperature.

Seth really did not want to climb down into that pit. That dark hole in the ground.

But it was the only way out. And they needed it now.

"Here, let me go first," he said to Laura, stepping around her so he could be the initial one to descend into the hopefully stable unknown. He stepped onto the ladder and climbed down. At least it felt secure, not shaking or creaking as he put his full weight on it. That was a good sign.

Once Seth reached the bottom, Laura handed Abby to him. Then she climbed down the ladder after him. Seth handed Abby back to Laura and climbed halfway up the ladder so he could close the closet door and then the trapdoor. He wished he had a way to cover up the entrance. Hopefully the assault team wouldn't find the hidden passage right away. He and Laura needed all the time they could get.

"Here, let me help." Seth was surprised to see that Laura had set Abby down. She climbed up the ladder with him and focused her light on where the door had closed. There was a latch. And a lock. Seth was suddenly grateful for paranoid men who built escape tunnels and thought to equip them with locks. They secured the door and climbed down.

Laura picked Abby back up and they turned

to face the tunneled path in front of them. Their flashlights only illuminated the space about ten feet ahead. It was dark and cold. Damp. Seth couldn't see the walls surrounding them, but he felt them. "Okay. Guess this is the only way to go now."

They headed into the black. Laura scanned the interior of the tunnel with her flashlight as they walked. "I haven't been in this thing for years. I played in it once or twice when I was a child, but Dad was always worried it wouldn't remain a secret tunnel if I kept using it. He was pretty big on separating toys from survival tools."

Seth really couldn't think of anything to say in response to that. He supposed that if he had been a recluse with a secret escape tunnel, he probably wouldn't have wanted a child playing in it, either. It made sense in a hermit sort of way.

"All right. This should take us out of here." Laura sounded more hopeful than confident. She turned and looked at Seth, bringing her flashlight with her so that they could see one another. The expression on her face was a mixture of triumph and fear.

Seth knew the feeling. It was currently residing in his own chest. They had made it out of the cabin. The men with guns did not know where they were right now. But Seth also didn't know where they would be in a few feet. "Where does the tunnel end? I mean, will we be far enough away?"

Laura shifted her hold on Abby. The little girl looked more alert. Her big dark eyes, so much like Laura's, were watching him. Laura kissed Abby on the cheek and looked at him to answer his question.

"It's really long. I don't know exactly how long. I just remember it seemingly going on for forever when I was a child. It comes out farther up the mountain. Closer to the top. I'm pretty sure we'll be safe. I mean, I hope we will be."

Pressure expanded in Seth's chest as he thought about the chance that she was wrong. That they would walk out of this tunnel into something worse than the men at the cabin. Or that they would end up trapped here by the fire. Seth took a deep breath, set his shoulders and started walking. There really wasn't anything else to do, and they were wasting time.

The tunnel wasn't wide enough for two adults to walk next to one another. Thankfully, though, it was tall enough that Seth could stand fully upright. It made him feel less like some kind of underground mole. Or troll. "I'll go first and try to shine my light so you can use it, too. That way you can hold Abby with both arms. The ground looks clear at least."

Laura was keeping up with Seth's pace as he spoke. He hoped she understood that the tunnel was safe only for as long as it took those men outside the cabin to come inside and find it. Once that happened, it would become a prison. Or a tomb.

Laura shuddered, as though reading his thoughts, and looked at Abby. She was clearly terrified for her daughter, focused solely on keeping Abby safe. No, Seth vowed to himself, this tunnel would not become a tomb. Seth increased his speed, grateful that Laura followed fast enough that he was still right in front of her.

"That door was metal, and the lock seemed sturdy." Seth knew he was trying to reassure himself just as much as he was Laura. He felt a bit like Pollyanna, trying to play the glad game. But his words were the truth and being optimistic always felt better than sitting in despair. "I'm not sure how prepared that team is, but I don't think they will have an easy time breaking through." He looked behind him and Laura jerked her head up and down once in a nod. "Your dad's paranoia is turning out to be a good thing."

Seth heard Laura's steps falter, but when he looked back her legs had resumed their prior movements. He'd regretted his words the moment he said them, but he regretted them even more when he saw that look in her eyes. It wasn't anger so much as sadness. Resignation. Seth didn't like the way that look made him feel. He breathed out through his nose, wondering why he couldn't have kept his judgment to himself. Criticizing her dad, a man she clearly loved, wasn't going to do a thing to help their situation. Moreover, he was the reason they still had a fighting chance against that army surrounding the cabin. *Lord, when will I ever learn?*

"He wasn't paranoid. Or crazy. Or a criminal." There wasn't any heat in her tone. Seth almost wished there had been. Surely hard anger would have been easier to digest than the resignation in her voice. Seth wasn't making her mad. He was hurting her.

He sighed. The man had been her father, so of course she would defend him. He didn't know what to say. He should apologize, but he still believed the words he was saying. He just wished they didn't upset Laura.

"My dad never hurt a soul in his entire life. All he wanted was to live on the mountain by himself. To be left alone. He never did anything bad to anyone, but people couldn't just let him be. They had to judge him. Question him. And make sure he knew that they considered him some kind of scary deviant."

She wasn't wrong. The stories of Old Man Grant were legendary in the park ranger office. They included tales of criminal behavior. But that behavior had been minor. Grant had not appreciated the restrictions governing use of public lands. Especially those pertaining to hunting or cutting down timber. He'd trapped animals and taken trees, but only what he needed to survive. At most, Grant was hostile. Rude. Protective of his land and more than a little frightening. Seth knew the conflict between Grant and the rangers in the office at the time had escalated to an unhealthy level on both sides.

A man who wanted to be alone. Much like Laura, it seemed. A man with a daughter. Also like Laura. "But he wasn't alone, was he? He had you for company. And your mother?" Seth was clearly prying for information. He couldn't help himself. He was speed walking through a tunnel, fleeing from an unknown threat, with a woman who had probably caused this mess to begin with. He was surprised by his curiosity, but it was a welcome distraction from what was behind them in the tunnel and what might be ahead.

Seth didn't want to get away from Laura. He wanted to know who she was and why she was on this mountain. She was also known for being hostile to the outside world. Why was that?

Seth wanted to know…her. Period. Laura didn't really fit with the vision of Old Man Grant's daughter.

"I think we better stop talking and save our energy. We're probably going to need it." Laura's voice sounded brittle. It seemed she was done talking.

Seth didn't say anything, but he did turn his attention fully on the stretch of tunnel in front of them. It had not changed in width or height but he thought he could feel it curving. Taking them somewhere.

He was walking in the dark. Again.

Seth had thought his days of battle were behind him. He had worked hard to put them there. Leaving the war had cost him everyone he had ever loved. Well, that wasn't exactly true. It was the way Seth refused to let his family help him after the war that had ruined everything.

Seth had so many regrets surrounding how he let war dominate his life. Now, it seemed, he had walked right back into it.

It was as awful as he remembered.

THREE

They walked and walked and walked. Hustling, Laura kept trying to listen over the sounds of their feet and breaths. She didn't know what she was listening for, exactly.

She thought she heard footsteps. Or voices. Or both. Her voice came out as a harsh whisper. "Do you hear something?"

Seth immediately stopped. He held up his hand, and Laura wanted to say that she didn't need him to tell her to be quiet. She didn't, though. As much as she did not want to be with Seth right now, she didn't want to be alone in the tunnel more. Well, not alone. Alone would be okay. It was meeting with a team of armed men dressed in black that she was looking to avoid.

Laura was glad she could hear Seth's ragged breathing as well as her own. It was nice to not be the only one feeling the pressure of this situation. Seth's whisper was soft, but not hesitant. "I don't hear anyone. I think we're still okay."

Laura looked at him and nodded. She readjusted Abby in her arms and jerked her head forward. Taking the hint, Seth started to move again. He might not have heard anything, but Laura noticed that his pace was slightly faster than it had been before she had asked her question. She was okay with walking faster.

This tunnel was not nearly as exciting and fun as Laura remembered. Instead of an adventure, the journey felt like a horror movie. She looked at Abby, who was dealing with this as though she went on trips through dark tunnels with her mommy every day. Laura made sure her grip on her daughter was firm and increased her pace, silently urging Seth along.

She had been frozen in the cabin. Unable to fully comprehend the danger, she had felt almost like she was sleepwalking. Now, however, her body thawed. She no longer felt like a statue. But it wasn't a relief. Instead of being frozen, her stomach was suddenly boiling with fear. Acid was bubbling, trying to burn its way up her throat. Her goose bumps were replaced with sweat. Her heart was beating again, but far too quickly. She tried to use Abby as an anchor, muffling a gasp into her sweet girl's hair.

She was probably scaring her daughter. Laura tried to stop. She couldn't.

When Seth suddenly turned and looked at her, Laura flinched. Her gasp must have given her away. He frowned and stopped mid-stride when she instinctively took the small step away from him. She didn't want to be weak. But, if she was, she definitely didn't want to be weak in front of him.

"Hey. Laura. It's going to be okay."

She looked at him like he had lost his mind, and he actually chuckled softly. "Okay, okay. It's not good. But we're not down yet, and I have faith." He smiled at her, his face warm and almost comforting. Then he continued walking down the tunnel.

Faith. Laura had faith. But faith wasn't always enough. Laura looked at her daughter and, as always, saw pieces of Josh. Abby's eyes were all Laura but Abby's dimples were all Josh. Tears welled up, and Laura closed her eyes as she kissed her daughter's head. Josh was dead from a mugging. Sometimes the evil in the world won. Laura swallowed, trying to clear her throat of the panic and excess saliva her now-burning body was creating.

Abby must have picked up on her mom's distress, because she reached those chubby hands up to frame Laura's face. Then she placed a smacking kiss on her mom's cheek, causing Laura to laugh out loud. Laura looked at Seth when she heard him chuckling, too. They shared a smile before Laura remembered that he wasn't her friend. No. He was one of those people who delighted in their supposed superiority over others.

Seth certainly wasn't the first person to say something disparaging about her dad. In fact, people had only bad things to say about the man who had shown her more love and acceptance in her life than she had ever found anywhere else. The man who had literally saved her life.

Josh had loved Laura. And Laura had loved him, and the family they created, in return. But the Laura who Josh met was relatively whole. She liked to think that it hadn't been too hard for her husband to fall for her. The daughter that Laura had been... Well that person was someone who was scared and hurt and bratty most of the time. And her dad had loved her in spite of it and during all of it. He had brought her through it.

Laura usually recognized that trying to defend her dad was a wasted effort. People saw Malcolm Grant—saw how he lived—and made their judgments. They weren't interested in the truth. They just wanted the most sensational story. They didn't care about the man who had survived in this world the best he knew how.

Her dad might have chosen to live apart from everyone, but he had been the best man Laura had ever met. He had sacrificed his solitude to raise her because he knew that she did not have any other family. Just him, an uncle who wanted to be alone. And her Uncle Malcom had put aside his wants for her needs and had become her dad. He deserved better. Laura couldn't keep quiet when people started telling the tale of Old Man Grant. If nothing else, the anger helped push away the loneliness. And Laura would much rather be angry than alone.

Her steps faltered and she squeezed Abby a bit too tight as she regained her footing. Seth turned to look.

"I'm fine. Keep going." He pressed his lips together, then turned and started on again without saying a word. Apparently, he didn't care for her demeanor just now. Too bad. Laura didn't care what he thought. So there. She viciously shoved down the guilt. This man was not her friend. He could not be her friend.

Even if she really needed one.

Nope. She wasn't going there. Not with this man. No matter how attractive he was. No matter how many times he was kind to her. She wasn't going there. She'd tried the real world once, and it had shattered every bit of her life.

"Does it feel like the tunnel is going up to you?"

Laura was startled by Seth's question. Embarrassed that she had been caught so deep in her thoughts, she suppressed a sharp retort. Snapping at him might feel good in the short term, but Laura would eventually regret it. Instead, she focused on the tunnel. On her feet and her senses, trying to discern whether they were moving deeper into the earth or coming up out of it.

"I… I think we are! Moving up, I mean." It might be her mind playing tricks on her, but the floor of the tunnel seemed to be sloping upward. It was slight, but there.

Laura looked ahead and laughed. There really was a light at the end of the tunnel. Or at least a sliver of something that wasn't dusty and dank.

They reached the door, and Seth pushed. The wood made some creaking noises, but nothing else happened. It did not open.

Laura set Abby down and focused her light on the latch, trying to give Seth enough illumination to hopefully figure out how to open it. Her headache had only worsened with all the emotional highs and lows of the last hour. It seemed as though her body was flooded with adrenaline or dread every ten minutes.

"It's stuck, isn't it?" Laura was trying to keep her tone even, aware of Abby's little ears.

Seth didn't turn to look at her, using both hands to fumble with the rusty latch. "It'll be okay. If I can't get the latch to work, then we'll break it down."

"Break it down?" Laura heard the doubt and hope in her own voice. Was everything in her life so contradictory?

Seth's hands paused, and he turned and gave Laura an arrogant smile, knocking on the door in front of them. "Yeah. This is a wood door. An old, wood door. We can handle this."

Laura wanted to believe him. She wanted to argue with him. Before she could do either, however, Seth spoke with smug satisfaction. "Got it."

He pushed the door again, and this time it gave an inch. Then, nothing. Again. Laura made a sound of frustration. She was surprised when Seth turned and put his hand on one of her shoulders, squeezing it lightly. "Hey, hey. It's okay. It looks like there's a bunch of foliage growing on the outside of the door. Vines or something."

Laura felt foolish. Of course. The tunnel door wasn't exactly used every day. Nature had done what it always does. It had persevered, covering the ground and taking back what had originally belonged to it. She needed to get a grip. "Sorry. You're right. I don't know why I'm acting like this, but I'm done. No more hysterics."

Seth laughed and squeezed her shoulder again before letting go. He was reaching into his pocket as he spoke. "You're not being hysterical. I grew up with three sisters. Sisters who were all teenagers at one point. Believe me, I know hysterical."

Laura knew her expression was rueful. He made it sound like teenage girls were torture. Which, they probably were to a brother.

"Besides, I'd say you have plenty of reason to be upset. I'm not exactly calm myself."

Laura appreciated his efforts to make her feel better. She watched with growing excitement as he used the pocketknife to cut the plants that were visible through the one-inch space that the door had opened. Once done, Seth closed the pocketknife and put it back in his pocket. He looked at Laura and Abby, smiled and pushed the door open.

They climbed out of that tunnel and walked into paradise. The sky was blue and the birds were singing. Laura could smell pine. It was a beautiful day. The kind of day for skipping and playing and laughing.

The wind blew, and Laura felt the tears threaten again. Smoke. She smelled smoke. Or at least she smelled the suggestion of smoke. She'd forgotten about why Seth said he came up her mountain, onto her land. "There really is a forest fire, isn't there?"

He was looking in the direction from which the wind had blown. Down the mountain. In between them and help. His voice was heavy with regret. "Yes, Laura. There really is a forest fire."

Seth's instincts were pushing against each other. The part of him concerned about a group of armed men coming out of the tunnel wanted to run down the mountain. Down meant people. Down meant safety. The part of him that did not want to get caught in a forest fire wanted to run up. Up meant no flames and no flashes of burning heat and no death by smoke inhalation. The one thing his warring intuition agreed on, however, was that they should not stand there and wait.

Seth heard Laura murmuring to Abby. He couldn't make out the words, but the tone was maternal and loving. He turned and shut the tunnel door. From the outside, the exit looked like a root cellar. He searched for a lock on the outside of the door, but there wasn't one. Old Man Grant's paranoia had apparently not gone far enough to encompass their current situation.

That was a shame.

Seth scanned the area and found some large fallen branches. Dragging them over to the door, he began to place them on top of it. He had just positioned the last branch when a small rock was tossed on top of his pile. Surprised, he looked up and saw Abby grinning at him. One chubby fist was empty and one was still gripping a small stone.

"I help," she said. She was beaming like she had welded the door shut.

Seth couldn't stop his smile. "Good job. You're a big help." His smile dimmed when he saw Laura walking toward them, struggling to carry a large boulder. Seth hurried to take it out of her arms.

She released it to him without a fight. "I thought some of these boulders would go well with your pile. They're certainly heavy enough."

Seth moved to place the boulder on top of the branches. Once he was done, Abby tossed her second rock. "One, two, three."

Seth laughed. "Yep. Three rocks. Let's get a few more, okay?"

Abby gave him a serious face. Or at least he thought it was supposed to be a serious face. "Get more." She started scanning the ground by her feet, exclaiming in delight when she found another pebble.

Seth went over to where Laura was, seeing several other large rocks. "Let's stack on a few more of these and then get moving. The weight will slow them down, but they'll get around it eventually."

Laura nodded, carrying a rock over and placing it in the pile. "Headed where? I'm not crazy about the idea of walking into a forest fire."

Her tone indicated that was an understatement.

"Me, neither. But we can't stay here. Those men will eventually figure out we're not inside the cabin. And since there are only so many places to search, they'll find the tunnel. We need to get far away from here." Seth looked into the forest as though that would provide some kind of answer.

Laura lifted her face and watched at him. Her expression wasn't exactly warm, but she didn't seem like she wanted to punch him again. That was probably a good sign.

Seth was comfortable in the woods. He was good at navigating them. Surviving in them. But this was Laura's mountain. She had grown up here. She was the one with the expertise right now. "We need a plan," he said. "Well, we need a safe place to go while we make a plan."

"What about the fire?"

Seth considered what he had seen of the

fire. The way the scent of smoke wafted on the air, just hinting at its existence. "I still think it's moving slow. Hopefully, firefighters are putting it out right now. Maybe it will end up being a nonissue. Or a way for us to find some emergency personnel to help us."

"It'll be dark soon. I don't know if that's a good thing or not, but night is coming." Laura was sounding like the practical and self-sufficient daughter of a mountain man. Seth liked it.

"We really need to get away from here," Seth said. "I don't like the idea of waiting around to see what comes out of that tunnel. Any ideas?" Seth was willing to consider just about anything at this point.

Laura stared up the mountain. "Maybe." A pause. "There's a creek not too far from here. Well, it's more like a river actually. If we walk on its banks, it should cover our tracks. Make us harder to find."

Seth felt savage satisfaction in his grin. "Yes. I like that idea. Lead the way," he said.

Laura picked Abby back up and started making her way through the forest.

"Do you want me to carry her? I don't mind." Seth asked the question to Laura's moving back.

"No. I've got her." Laura answered to the trees in front of her, not slowing or turning around. She was heading into a part of the forest that looked just like—well—every other part of the forest. Seth was suddenly very thankful. If he had to be trapped on a burning mountain with an assault team after him, at least it was with a woman who was raised in this wilderness.

Seth tried to think through their next steps, but he needed help. "Once we get there, we'll have to decide whether to go up or down the creek."

Laura turned around, surprise on her face. "What?"

"The creek. We'll have to decide which way to walk."

Laura continued through the trees. Her voice was contemplative when she spoke. "We can take the creek for a mile or so— long enough to lose any trackers. There's a place upstream where we should be able to get out without leaving too much evidence."

Seth nodded even though Laura couldn't see it. "That sounds good. Then what?"

"I know of a shelter not too far off. It was a place my dad used when he was hunting and didn't want to come all the way back to the cabin. It's sparse, but it's well hidden and has supplies."

"I like the sound of hidden and supplies." He hoped those supplies included weapons and ammunition. His service weapon was not going to provide a lot of protection against an armed team.

"I think I should head there with Abby."

Seth jolted. "You? With Abby?"

Laura did not turn around and look at him. "Yeah." She went on as though that was not a startling statement. "The creek is just over this rise."

Seth heard the creek before he saw it. It was perfect. Active enough to cover their tracks but shallow enough on the edges to allow them to walk without getting soaked.

They started trekking upstream, making sure to stay where the water would cover their tracks. Abby was watching the water, pointing at something every once in a while.

Laura spoke quickly, blurting her words out in a torrent of emotion. "Look. These guys are after me." She glanced at Abby, and the anguish on her face hurt Seth. "And Abby."

Seth waited. He did not see how agreeing with her would help anything. Laura continued, still talking quickly, her voice thick with sentiment. "You should go. You can probably make it back to town safely, especially if you're not with me. You don't need to get caught up in this."

Seth stopped walking. There was no way he could process what she had just said and keep moving at the same time. She thought he would leave her to save himself.

Filled with disgust at the very idea, Seth's voice was now heavy with emotion. "I'm not leaving you alone. I don't care what makes the most sense—I'm not leaving you two alone. We're going to get out of this mess together."

Laura looked at him. Oh, how he wished he could read that expression in her dark eyes. Did she believe him?

She opened her mouth, but Seth cut her off, angry that she thought he would be so cowardly as to save himself while letting a woman and child die. "No. I will march back to that tunnel and try to take care of that assault team by myself before I leave you two out here alone. We're all going to the shelter. We're all going to make a plan. We're all going to make it out of this."

She still looked like she wanted to argue. "Besides," he said, "they were watching the cabin and saw both me and my truck. They know we were in there together, and I'm sure they think you told me everything. I'm as big a liability as you are at this point."

Laura's voice was soft, but not defeated or angry. For that, at least, Seth was thankful. "All right. The shelter is this way."

They left the creek at the designated spot and headed up the mountain. Seth's legs started to burn after just a few minutes. He looked at Laura in front of him, Abby's arms wrapped around her neck.

Seth wanted to reach out and put his hand on Laura's shoulder to stop her but was afraid of destroying the fragile trust they seemed to have built. Instead he quit walking and coughed. Laura paused and turned to look at him. She had a question in her eyes, and he struggled to find the right words. "This is pretty rough terrain."

She waited, watching him. Probably wondering why he had stopped their progress to state the obvious. Seth felt himself becoming flustered, which made him want to snap. *No. That approach wasn't going to work.* He decided to just say it and wait for the rejection. "I was wondering if you wanted me to carry Abby for a little bit. She has to be getting heavy."

Laura looked at Abby, who seemed to be following the conversation with her sweet dark eyes. "She's been sick all week. I thought her fever had broken but it felt like it was coming back when I was carrying her in the tunnel. Are you sure you want to risk it?"

Seth couldn't stop the laugh. "I'm pretty sure, all things considered, getting the flu is the least of my worries right now."

Laura looked up at the sloping forest in front of them. She kissed Abby on the check and held her out toward Seth. "Thank you. A break would be nice."

Seth took the little girl, surprised at how light she felt. She was warm and wound her arms around his neck without hesitation. Laura began walking again, and Seth followed. The daylight was fading, and they needed to find a safe place to make it through the night. And they needed a plan for getting past both a forest fire and a group of armed men. *Help us to make the right choice, Lord. I don't want to let them down.*

FOUR

He was carrying her daughter. A park ranger was carrying her daughter. Her dad would be having a conniption right about now. This unexpected liaison with a park ranger was the most rebellious thing she'd ever done. Then again, Laura had never really had a rebellious phase. It was kind of hard to rebel when you lived alone on a mountain with a man who refused to get angry. She actually smiled at the thought of her father's face if he could see this.

"Mommy!"

Laura almost stumbled as she stopped and spun around. She should have known better than to place Abby in the hands of a park ranger. And then she had turned her back on them, not even watching what was going on.

The tension in her body evaporated as

Abby blew her a wet-sounding kiss, Duckie clutched in her arm. "Wuv Mommy! Mwah!"

Abby wasn't hurt. She wasn't in danger. She was cradled in Seth's arms, grinning with those chubby little cheeks, and then sending big kisses to her mom. Seth's huge smile faded as he looked at Laura. That handsome joy was replaced with an expression Laura couldn't name. Defensiveness? Disappointment? He had surely read the accusation on her face when she had turned around.

Whatever it was, it made Laura look away from Seth's face. She focused her gaze just above Abby's head as she forced a smile.

"I love you, too, baby."

Her face felt too tight, and it was hard to maintain the upward curve of her lips. Abby seemed to buy the act, however, as she turned back to Seth and started babbling. Something about leaves and rainbows.

Laura chanced a glance at Seth. He was watching her, his face impassive. Unable to maintain his gaze, she turned to face forward again, navigating the path almost subconsciously as she thought about the man behind her. She couldn't figure him out. No, that wasn't true. Laura couldn't figure herself out.

"How far away do you think the shelter is?"

His voice was conversational, almost as though he was asking how she liked her coffee. Laura kept walking, trying to keep her pace steady. She was grateful for his effort at normalcy, but she didn't want to see that look in his eyes again.

"If I'm remembering right, it should be up here about three miles or so." Laura was proud of how evenly she answered him. She felt like a little girl playing dress up with a neighbor boy—both pretending to be mature and sophisticated. Two grand adults having a lofty conversation in adult voices about adult things.

A confident adult was the last thing Laura felt like right now. She might not physically be a child anymore, but right now she was scared and confused. But she knew she wasn't alone, no matter how much it felt like it.

Laura swallowed hard as a smile fought with the impulse to cry. She had God. She had Abby. And she had a park ranger.

They walked. And walked. Laura thought the forest fire had maybe moved to the muscles of her legs, concentrating its burn there.

"It's pretty up here." Seth's voice was still conversational, as though they had been talking the entire time. Two people out for a stroll, enjoying the scenery. Laura wanted to thank him for his effort, but that would kind of defeat the purpose of making this situation seem ordinary.

"Yes, it is." Laura didn't have to try too hard to infuse her words with warmth. It was the truth. "I love this mountain. I'm sure part of that is because it's home. But really, who wouldn't look at all this and fall in love?" Laura took a second and gave the scenery the respect it deserved. She had been focusing on escape. On next steps. On routes and plans and maps that existed only in her memory. Now she was focusing on the masterpiece that God had created. The one she had missed desperately when she lived in Denver.

The trees had brown, textured trunks and lush green leaves and sharp, precise needles, and they burst with life. The forest floor was covered in leaves and plants, a soft carpet. Moss looked soft and inviting. Rocks seemed to pop up here and there, little chunks of sculpture decorating the land.

The wind was blowing away from them, and Laura tried to find the familiar scent of the forest. She wanted to smell pine and wood and that musty, tangy, thick mountain smell. It was there. Along with the faintest hint of smoke, unfortunately. But she couldn't see smoke yet, and that made her feel better. The sky was a color that, if she painted it, would probably be called unrealistic.

Laura's pace had slowed considerably. She felt herself begin to blush as she stopped her staring and resumed their original steady pace. She hadn't meant to get so caught up, but she also didn't want that horrible silence to return. She turned and gave Abby a big smile. "The mountain is pretty, isn't it, Abby McDabby?"

Abby looked at her and smiled right back. "Pretty! Pretty mountain."

Laura looked at Seth. His eyes were warm. Happy. Not wanting to ruin the moment and lose the feeling of hope that was growing in her chest, Laura faced front again. She took a deep breath, and let it out slowly.

Thank You, God. We needed this.

Feeling reassured and rejuvenated, Laura checked her surroundings to make sure that they were still on the right path. The break from reality was nice, but getting lost was the last thing they needed. Seth must have noticed her change in demeanor.

"Um, we're not lost, are we?" He sounded hesitant. That made Laura smile. He seemed afraid the question would anger her. And scared that they might, indeed, be lost. Still basking in the relief of the carefree atmosphere they had created, she tried to make her voice as serious as possible.

"Lost? Umm...noooo. I just don't see the tree where we need to turn."

Silence. Then, still hesitantly, "Tree?"

Laura was glad she was still in front of Seth. There was no way she would have been able to maintain a straight face. "Yeah. When we see this tree, then we need to make a hard left." She made of show of slowing her pace and looking at the nearly identical trees that surrounded them in the forest.

This time, his voice held a hint of dread. "What does the tree look like?"

Laura had to swallow quickly to keep the laugh inside. She waited a second until she thought her voice wouldn't give her away. Trying to sound as confident and nonchalant as possible, she responded, "It's tall. It has green leaves. The bark is a sort of brownish color."

Laura wished she could see Seth's face right now. He wasn't saying anything, and her mind was supplying all kinds of ideas about what his face might look like. His voice was decidedly thicker when he finally spoke. "Is there anything else? Anything that would make the tree stand out?"

Laura pretended to think for a second. "Oh! It does have some distinctive things on it."

"Distinctive? What are they?" Seth sounded relieved.

"It has moss on the trunk. Toward the bottom. And there are bird nests in the branches. And these squirrels. These certain squirrels live in it. They have bushy tails."

Laura heard Seth stop walking behind her. She put on her best poker face and turned to face him. "Is something wrong?"

Seth was looking at her with an expression that was probably half suspicion and half frustration. "Are you messing with me? We're looking for a tree that looks exactly like every other tree in this forest?"

Laura had to face the front and start walking again. She couldn't help but smile at how disgruntled Seth was. "I mean, they look different to me. But, then again, this is my mountain." Laura continued her pace. She hoped that Seth would follow.

"Mama!" Laura turned to see Abby pointing at her. Abby wasn't upset, but she clearly wanted Seth to keep up.

With a huge sigh, Seth started moving again. "You're messing with me. You have got to be messing with me." He sounded like he was trying to convince himself. "You are messing with me, right?"

Laura's tone was probably giving her away, but she was enjoying this too much to stop now. "Messing with you? Oh, you mean about what the tree looks like?"

Laura heard a humph from behind and almost giggled. "I'm not messing with you. I mean, how else would I know where to go? There aren't any street signs or anything like that." She wasn't exactly telling a lie. Laura's dad had taught her about finding her way on the mountain, and part of that involved looking at the trees. Knowing the forest by sight. Though he never put stock in memorizing where the squirrels with bushy tails were.

"So, we're looking for a special tree that is somehow different from all the other trees because it has bark and leaves and moss and nests and squirrels, even though every single tree I look at has all these things?"

Laura turned her laugh into a small cough. "Well, I don't know that I would call the tree special. I mean, isn't all of nature special?"

When Seth didn't respond, Laura's curiosity was too strong to ignore. She turned to see him muttering to Abby. He looked exasperated, but whatever he was saying was making Abby smile.

They rounded another tight clump of trees, and Laura realized that her fun was over.

"This is it. We're here."

Seth looked around, but "here" looked like every other place they had been since they got out of that tunnel. He was fairly certain that she was making fun of him. She had to be. She couldn't really be looking for a special squirrel tree. No. She was playing him. Probably.

Seth didn't normally enjoy being the butt of other people's jokes, but he found that he wasn't really upset with Laura. For one thing, he had seen her smile. Just for a second, but it was enough. Her cheeks had been pushed full, her eyes had seemed to come out from the shadows and she'd looked ten years younger. Seth had felt better, too.

Putting Abby down, he tried to discern where the shelter might be. He failed.

He looked to see Abby picking a flower that was growing near her feet and Laura standing there with her hands on her hips.

The smile was still in place, though. So was the amused expression she had been wearing and trying to hide for the last ten minutes.

Seth threw his hands up in the air in a gesture of defeat. "Okay, okay. I give. Tell me your terms, and I'll surrender."

Laura looked like she was pressing her lips together, and the corners of her mouth were slightly curved upward. Oh, yeah, she was teasing him. She walked over to a group of bushes and pulled some vines away.

There was a door.

In the middle of the forest.

There was a door in the middle of the forest.

Seth was stunned. Yet, he had known somehow that Laura would come through for them.

The door looked old and rickety. As he walked toward it, Seth realized that the clump of bushes was not really a bunch of bushes growing together. Instead, it was a building of some sort. The shelter.

Seth walked inside, pulling out a flashlight from his belt as he did so. The interior of the cabin was similar to Laura's rustic cabin, though much smaller. It was basically just a room. The fireplace surprised Seth because he definitely didn't remember seeing a chimney outside. Of course, he didn't see the building, either. Seth spotted two windows, both with interior shutters closed over them. Seth guessed that if he opened the shutters, he would only see the dense brush that was covering the cabin. He noted a bed, a table with chairs and a kitchen that looked like it belonged on a campsite.

"Secret fort!"

Abby's excited voice drew Seth's attention to the door. She was pulling against Laura's hand, trying to get inside while her mother just stood in the doorway and watched Seth.

"It sure looks like a secret fort, doesn't it, Abby?" Seth was glad Abby was excited instead of scared. So far, she seemed to be calm or acting like she was on a grand adventure. Seth hoped it could stay that way. He didn't want the little girl to be afraid.

"Well, it's not much." Laura sounded resigned, like she had expected the worst and the worst is what they had gotten.

"It's perfect," Seth said. "It's hidden. It's dry." He opened cupboard and closet doors as he walked around the room, noting the precious supplies they held. "And it's got supplies." He was relieved to see a rifle with ammunition. He'd take that with him when they left.

Laura looked behind her, out into the open forest and then closed the door. "Do you think they are tracking us?"

Seth considered it for a moment. "I'm sure they will, eventually. But those men had a very urban look, Laura. I doubt they spend a whole lot of time in the wilderness."

Laura didn't look convinced.

"Even if they do, we have you," Seth said. She looked surprised. Maybe shocked that he was giving her a compliment. "You know these woods. You knew how to get us to this shelter with minimal evidence left behind." Seth recalled standing right in front of the shelter, knowing it was nearby, and still being unable to detect it. "And you led us to a shelter that is about as hidden in plain sight as something can be. In fact—" Seth stopped as the sound of a helicopter filled the small cabin.

Almost as one, they ran to the front door. Laura was reaching out, preparing to pull it open and run outside when Seth's hand on her arm stopped her. "No, Laura. Wait."

"What if it's help?" She sounded desperate. It hurt to hear.

"What if it's not?"

That did it. Laura dropped her hand and just stared at the door. Seth didn't have time to think. The chopper sounded like it was passing overhead right now. He needed to get a look at it. Barely cracking the door, Seth saw the chopper flying in the direction of Laura's cabin.

"Seth?" Laura's voice made some of the tightness leave his face. He carefully shut the door and turned to face her.

"That was not a police or fire chopper. It looked private. All black."

Still frozen, Laura tried to get her tongue to work. "More men?"

Seth met her eyes. "Maybe. Or Mahoney's escape plan. But they didn't see us. Nothing has really changed."

Laura sighed. Seth didn't know if she was reassured or had just decided talking wasn't going to help anything. "Okay, so what now?"

Seth opened the door to peek out again. The sun was setting. "It's going to be dark soon. I think we should spend the night here. Rest, gather supplies."

Laura looked like she was going to argue. "What about the fire?" she asked. "I really don't want to wake up surrounded by flames."

It was a valid fear. And Seth didn't know anything for sure. "I think we'll be okay for now. I still think it's moving slow."

Laura looked at him, her face screaming that she was entirely unconvinced.

"Laura, I'll do whatever you want, okay? If you think we should keep moving, we will. But right now we just smell smoke. We don't see it and we don't see flames. None of our choices are good. But I think we should hide and rest for a bit."

Laura nodded. "We should go ahead and seal ourselves inside here as best we can. Try to hide the shelter as much as possible in case they come by."

Seth agreed, grateful that she was trusting his plan. Of course, that also meant anything that went wrong would be on him. A sharp pain shot across Seth's jaw and he realized he was clenching it.

There were no good choices, he reminded himself. They just needed to do their best.

Laura opened doors and drawers, much as Seth had done earlier. When she found a doll and a set of large blocks, she gave them to Abby. Abby promptly sat on the bed and began playing quietly.

Seth raised his eyebrows at the find. Looking at him, Laura smiled sheepishly. "Those were mine. Dad liked to keep me busy. I was quieter when I was busy."

"I bet." Seth pictured a rustic mountain man taking a little girl along on his excursions.

Laura went back to her exploration of the cupboards. She pulled several cans out and rummaged until she found a can opener. "Well, we'll have something to eat at least." She looked at the fireplace and then at Seth. "I don't think we should start a fire. The smoke would be a dead giveaway."

"Agreed."

Laura opened the first can and smelled the contents. Seemingly satisfied, she dumped the contents into a bowl. "I hope you like pork and beans. Cold."

Seth thought about some of the meals he had eaten in Afghanistan. "That sounds perfect."

Laura filled three bowls, found three spoons and they sat down at the table to eat. Even though they were near strangers, on the run, hiding in the woods and eating cold pork and beans, the meal reminded Seth of home. Of eating with his family at the kitchen table. He felt a pang of longing.

Seth was brought from his thoughts by Abby grabbing his hand. Her other fist gripped her mother's hand. Laura held out her free hand toward Seth's. Her voice was quiet. Tentative. "Um, we always hold hands and pray before we eat."

Feeling a little foolish for not realizing earlier, Seth took Laura's hand.

Laura looked at Abby. "Go ahead, honey."

Abby closed her eyes and bent her head down. Seth did the same. "Dear God, thank You. Amen."

Seth smiled and looked over to see Laura's sheepish smile. "Her prayers are a little…short." She sounded amused and almost embarrassed.

Seth looked at Abby and patted her on the back. "That was great, Abby. I like a woman who knows how to be concise and efficient."

Abby smiled at Seth, likely not understanding all of his words but knowing she was loved and adored. She quickly remembered the food and concentrated on eating her dinner. Seth took a bite, pleased to find that the meal, while simple and cold, was actually quite good. "This is delicious. Thank you."

Laura chuckled. "All I did was open a can, but you're welcome."

After eating dinner, Laura put Abby to bed

and then sat across from Seth at the table. The old oil lamp Laura had produced from somewhere made a nice glow. If it weren't for the armed men coming after them, this could have been a fun camping trip. Seth had certainly spent worse nights in his life.

Laura's voice was low when she spoke. Seth wondered whether it was because she didn't want to wake Abby or because of the subject of her question. "What are we going to do if they find us?" Laura turned her head and looked at Abby. Seth saw tears glistening in her eyes before she faced him again. "What are we going to do if they don't find us?"

Seth didn't want to give her platitudes about roses and bunnies. She was an adult. She was a mother. She needed to hear the truth and to know the risks of all their options. But, first, Seth needed to figure out what their options were. He wasn't exactly coming up with a long list.

"I don't honestly know, Laura."

"The smell of the smoke lessened as we walked to the shelter, I think. But that could have been the wind. Do you think we've walked far enough away from the fire?"

"I'm a little turned around after our adventure as moles, but we're farther up the mountain now than we were before, aren't we?"

Laura nodded.

"Okay. So when I saw the fire it was definitely spreading in such a way that it will block all attempts to get down this side of the mountain. The wind could change but—"

"We can't go down."

"Well, there's a chance that crews are fighting the fire right now. That if we walked toward the flames we'd also be walking toward help. But that risk makes me nervous. So I'd say the shortest route to help is probably out. I would hate to try it, hoping the fire won't block us, and then find out it is. I don't like that scenario at all."

Laura's gaze was steady. "And the men with guns might still be out there. Looking for us."

"Yes." Seth wanted to lie to her. But he respected her enough to give her the truth, even though he hated the expression that crossed her face. She looked, well, trapped. And it was a horrible thing to see on another person's face.

"How do you feel about us staying here?" Laura asked. "We have enough food for a couple of weeks. Maybe longer if we ration it. If it came down to it, I could leave to hunt. It feels safe here."

Seth thought about her question, appreciating the way she was treating him. The war between the park rangers assigned to this area and her family was almost mythical. But she was not digging into the conflict. Instead, she was dealing with the here and now. And, in this here and now, they needed to work together to get out alive. To get Abby out alive.

Seth froze when he thought he heard something outside. He had barely formed the thought when Laura extinguished the lamp and moved over to the bed where Abby slept. She had heard it, too, which meant it was real.

Seth knew there was a full moon and a sky full of stars out there. Bright and beautiful. He'd walked through the forest on nights like this before and had never even needed to pull out his flashlight. The cabin was completely dark, though, so overgrown on the outside that no light came in.

The sound outside became louder and more distinct. Something coming through the brush, breaking branches and crunching the leaves and needles that made up the forest floor. And voices. Male voices, loud and aggressive.

"This is pointless. We're wandering around in the dark getting eaten alive by mosquitoes for no reason. They could be anywhere."

"Shut your mouth. Boss says to get them— we get them."

Seth looked at the dark shapes that were Laura and Abby on the bed. He wanted to go over there. He wanted to wrap his arms around them and use his body as a shelter. He stayed where he was, though. He was afraid that he would bump into something or knock something over if he tried to get to them in the dark. The last thing they needed was for him to alert these guys of their location.

Instead, Seth looked at the door. Or, where he thought the door was. He thanked God that he still had his gun on him. He hoped he would not need it, but he felt better having it in his hand.

Seth stopped breathing when a small beam of light came inside the cabin. The men had powerful flashlights. And the cabin wasn't as protected from outside eyes as he had thought.

FIVE

The small beam of light almost danced as it moved along the far cabin wall. If Abby had been awake, she would have probably laughed in delight. That light should be beautiful. Instead, it made Laura feel like she was going to vomit.

"Yeah, well, I don't care what the boss says. If I see a bear, I'm getting out of here."

The man's voice was louder than before. Closer. Laura wanted to cradle Abby to her body, but she didn't dare wake the sleeping child. Abs was a heavy sleeper, but Laura was poised to hush her if it looked like she was starting to stir.

"Why are we even here? I'm telling you, man, they went down the mountain."

"Boss says the fire would have stopped them."

The light left the cabin. Where were they going?

"Then they're in the middle of the fire, nice and crispy. Why are we looking for dead people?"

Laura winced. The man sounded pleased at the thought of three people burning to death.

"Yeah, well, this is pointless."

"I heard you the first time. I don't want to hear it a third. Boss has us split up, covering the entire mountain. We'll find them. And, when we do, she's gonna watch her daughter die. Then she and that ranger are gonna get it, too. They've made this hard enough. Boss is done with accidental and humane."

The voices had been decreasing in volume as the men were hopefully walking away, but Laura clearly heard that last part. She swallowed rapidly several times, trying to fight the urge to vomit, which had become almost unstoppable as those men talked about hurting Abby. Hurting her sweet little girl who couldn't even conceive of such evil.

It was silent outside, but no one moved inside the cabin. Laura put a hand over her stomach, willing it to calm down. There was a time and place for everything, and this was neither the time nor the place for her to have a breakdown. She needed to save her daughter, then she could worry about hysterics.

When she felt like she had control over her body again, Laura looked at Seth. Well, she looked in the direction she had last seen him. He had been utterly silent ever since she had blown out the light, so Laura assumed he was still at the table. She would have heard him move.

Was he was looking at her, too? What was he doing? How long should they wait until those guys were out of earshot? Were more coming?

The questions were flying in Laura's head, and she realized her hands were squeezed into fists. No. No, no, no. She forced her fingers to relax and folded them together. She slid to her knees on the ground without making a sound and kneeled next to Abby's sweet little sleeping body. Laura leaned over, closed her eyes and began to pray.

It was a familiar prayer. Her favorite saying was one about why worry if you pray and why pray if you are going to worry. Laura loved that saying, but it was also her nemesis of sorts. She prayed. She tried to give her burdens to God. Truly. But, no matter how good her intentions, she always kept the worry. She obsessed. She planned. It made her prayers feel like a mockery and inevitably started a cycle of worrying and praying about worrying and worrying about worrying while praying.

But Laura still tried. Because when it came down to it, Abby was going to learn by watching what Laura did. No matter what Laura said. So Laura kept on trying. She prayed about her worries. And she prayed that God would help her release them to Him.

Here, in this dark cabin, Laura felt very much alone. Out of control. And absolutely terrified. So she leaned over her daughter, turned her fists into hands of prayer and tried to talk to her Heavenly Father. It was working, too. She was still anxious, but the absolute panic was fading. God was in control. God was in control. God was in control.

"I'm coming your way." Laura jumped at his whisper, but was thankful for the warning. She was so focused that she might have screamed if Seth appeared next to her without telling her first. He didn't make a sound as he crossed the room, and Laura didn't know he was there until she felt his warmth next to her. He placed his hands over hers.

"I'd like to pray with you, if that's okay?"

"Is it safe?" It felt almost sacrilegious worrying that they both should not pray at the same time. But practicality won out again. Shouldn't one of them be watching the door? Maybe they should pray in shifts. The thought made a wave of hysterical laughter bubble in Laura's throat, but she suppressed it.

Of course it was safe to pray. Especially now. This man wanted to pray with her. He wasn't scorning her for praying in such a dire situation. He wasn't being cynical about her prayer. No, he wanted to join her.

"Of course you can. I have to warn you, though. I'm not very good at this. I never have been. It seems that practice doesn't make perfect in my case."

Seth squeezed her hands, and this time his voice was slightly chiding. "Hey, don't do that. Don't be all self-deprecating. I'm scared, too. I was grateful when I realized you were praying, because I really need it, too."

"I, um…" Laura really didn't know how to respond to that. She went back to bowing her head, looking away from Seth's face, which was still hidden in shadows. Here, in the dark, it seemed intimate, yet right, that they should hold hands and pour out their fears together.

They didn't say anything, just interlaced

their fingers. Kneeled side by side. Shared warmth and communion. Laura's mind calmed. Her body strengthened. She breathed out an "Amen" and looked up at Seth as he did the same. She removed her hands from his and pulled the covers back up around Abby as she slept.

Seth stood and moved to the cabin door. The longer they stayed in the complete darkness, the more Laura was able to see. Seth's eyes must have been adjusting the same way because he did not seem to stumble. Laura watched him put his ear near the door, though he was definitely a shadowed figure instead of a clear person.

He moved to the shuttered windows and did the same thing. Then he came back to where Laura was still sitting on the floor next to the bed. "I think they're gone. I don't think they realized we were here."

"But they are going to keep looking, aren't they? Mahoney really wants us dead."

Seth crouched down, sitting back on his heels so that he was about face level with her. "Yes. It sounded like they are going to keep looking until they find us."

Laura noted that he said *us*. And he was right. He was in this now. She had done this to her daughter and to him. She was the one who finally felt ready to go through all the boxes of her husband's things. She was the one who had found the key. And somehow she was the reason Mahoney knew about the key. She had to be. Laura didn't know how Mahoney knew. But she found the key and less than a week later he was here. This was all her fault. Even though she had just prayed, she still felt helpless. That feeling of not being able to do anything to change an awful situation rose up again.

Like when her parents died. Like when Malcolm, her second dad, died. Like when Josh died.

Laura put her hands down on the bed and felt Abby.

Abby.

And she sniffled back a laugh. Yes, she had been in many horrible, helpless places before in her life. Circumstances that she couldn't change, no matter how hard she prayed and wished and tried. But God had brought her through. Had given her a new father. A daughter. Reasons to keep going and ways to smile and laugh even after she'd sworn she'd never do either again.

Seth came back and Laura looked at him

from her place on the floor. "What do you think we should do?"

"We need to sleep. We won't be any good in the morning if we're both exhausted."

That was a good plan in theory. In reality, though, Laura knew she would never be able to sleep with a forest full of armed men looking for her. And her baby. "I won't be able to sleep."

Instead of arguing with her, Seth just nodded his head. Laura liked how he did not dismiss her concerns as trivial. "I agree. I'd be too afraid of waking up with a gun pointed at my face."

Laura cringed at his bluntness. She really didn't need an image to go along with her fear.

Seth looked at the door and nodded. "Here's the plan. We'll take turns keeping watch and sleeping. We have about seven hours until daylight. You go to sleep now. I'll wake you up in a few hours and then I'll sleep."

It wasn't a bad plan. "You'll really wake me up? I'm going to be mad if you let me sleep all night and you stay awake." Laura wanted to get out of this alive more than she wanted chivalry. She was going to need Seth alert and awake tomorrow.

His smile was rueful in an adorable kind of way that confused Laura. "I'll wake you up. My goal is to keep you and Abby safe, and I need to get at least a few hours shut-eye to make that happen."

"Okay." Laura climbed into the bed with Abby, pulling the small child to her and smiling when little arms and legs automatically curled around her even though Abby was sound asleep. Laura saw Seth move closer to the door and sit on the floor, leaning against the wall. He didn't light the lamp again.

She closed her eyes and tried to breathe slowly and evenly, but gave up after a couple of minutes. She stared at the black of the ceiling and tried to listen to the forest, the sounds that had been her lullaby since the day Malcolm Grant took her out of that hospital. She only heard her blood roaring in her ears.

"Seth?" she whispered, hoping he would hear her.

"Yeah?"

"What are we going to do in the morning?"

He didn't answer right away, and tears rose in Laura's throat.

"When it's light outside, we'll make a plan. It'll be a new day."

Oddly, that helped. A new day. Yes. Things

often looked better in the morning. Laura closed her eyes and slept.

Seth woke up and had absolutely no idea where he was. That never happened. Whether in the desert, in his bed or camping in the forest, Seth always woke up and knew exactly where he was.

But not today. There was someone in the bed with him. He blinked and tried to figure out where in the world he was. And how he got there.

Then he remembered. His eyes popped open and he saw the warm body next to him. Abby. She was on top of the covers while he was under them, but he still felt heat coming from her small form. And she had a little hand thrown across his chest, little finger slightly curled.

He turned his head and saw Laura smiling at him. She waved hello. Still slightly off-balance, Seth just waved back.

It was daylight. From the brightness inside the cabin, it had to be well after sunrise. Laura was standing at the little table doing something with cans and plates. Seth sat up and slowly moved away from the little girl, doing his best to not wake her. He folded the covers over her as he got up.

He walked over to where Laura was preparing breakfast of some sort. His stomach growled, and he knew he'd be grateful for the food even if it was more cold pork and beans. He looked at his watch. Eight thirty. He'd woken Laura up around three in the morning, hoping to get at least a couple of hours of sleep before sunrise.

He'd overslept. On the run from too many bad guys to count, stuck in a hobbit fortress, a forest fire probably coming their way and he'd overslept. Unbelievable.

"Why didn't you wake me?" He tried not to sound too accusing, but he was definitely having a surreal morning and that carried through to his tone of voice. Laura stopped what she was doing to look at him.

"I'm sorry. You and Abby were sleeping so soundly. I watched the sunrise and just felt," she paused and looked away, a blush rising on her cheeks, "peaceful. This is a peaceful place. I wasn't in a hurry to wake you and have reality come back to slap me in the face."

Seth understood that. He did. And he certainly felt better after five hours sleep than he would have after two and a half. Besides, they were probably about as safe in this cabin as they could be, given the current circumstances. "I'm sorry, Laura. I get that. I didn't mean to sound like I was mad at you."

She smiled a grateful little smile that made his heart feel funny, then went back to creating breakfast out of hermit survivalist rations.

"How did Abby get in the bed?" This time his tone was all curiosity. He'd woken Laura and prepared to bunk on the floor, leaving the bed for the little girl. Laura had refused. To the point of almost yelling at him even though they were trying to be as quiet as possible. She'd picked Abby up and said she was going over by the door to keep watch and to snuggle with her baby and he better get his butt in bed.

Seth almost laughed as he remembered. Laura Donovan was fierce and more than a little scary when she got going. Which shouldn't surprise him too much since their introduction involved her punching him in the face.

Abby had slept through the entire thing, as content to sleep in her mama's lap as she had been in the bed. Seth wondered about that kind of trust. He had known it once. The knowledge that you don't have to worry, because there was someone there to take care of you. He was overcome by the intense longing to make sure the sweet child stayed that way for as long as possible. He vowed internally that this little girl was going to come off this mountain with that innocence intact. Yes, she was.

He was also a little worried. Abby had slept for a good chunk of their journey so far. Seth knew it was because she was sick. Laura had told him it was just a cold, just a slight fever. But she still deserved to recover in a nice bed. In a nice house. Free of the threat of violence.

"I put her down in the bed around sunrise," Laura said. "I'm sorry if she bothered you. I thought it would be okay since she was on top of the covers. And there seemed to be enough room."

"It was fine. I didn't even know she was there until I woke up." Seth wasn't upset about what Laura had done, but he was shocked. Yesterday, he was the enemy park ranger. He'd had to talk her into letting him carry Abby even though Laura was exhausted. But today? Today she put her precious daughter with him.

Seth felt something like pride in his chest

at the development. It was ridiculous, but he took it as a sign that she was beginning to trust him. To see him as one of the good guys. It had been a long time since Seth had felt proud of his character, but he did today. Laura thought he was a good man.

Please, Lord, let that be true. The plea was sudden and startling. He hadn't consciously thought it, but it leaped out of his soul. A cry for help, still waiting for an answer. The blanket of shame and regret Seth carried with him, the one that covered him and smothered him, lessened for a moment. He could breathe. Feel hope.

He'd been physically hurt in a war and then had hurt his family in return. Only, he'd hurt them emotionally instead of physically, which was almost worse. Then he'd left them, wounding them even more. Seth had somehow maneuvered himself into a dark corner with no light and no way out. It felt familiar to the current situation.

And yet he was starting to find hope.

Seth realized Laura was staring at him, and his ears started to burn. Yeah, he probably looked like a fool. Or a crazy man. She was probably back to wondering whether he was a reliable friend or not. "Sorry. I was just thinking. Can I help you?"

"I'm not sure there's much to do. I found some protein bars, but they look a couple years old. They haven't expired yet but that doesn't mean much when it comes to survival food. I thought we could take them with us. I also found some canned fruit. It didn't have an expiration date, and it smells okay. So…" Laura's voice trailed off.

"So, we're having fruit surprise for breakfast and bricks for lunch," Seth finished for her.

Laura laughed, a glorious sound that belied the danger they were in. "Pretty much. I'm going to wake Abby." She took a couple of steps toward the bed. Stopped. "She'll have to go to the bathroom when she wakes up. Do you think it's safe to go outside?"

Abby wasn't the only one who needed a little privacy. "I'll go check it out. I'll be back." He picked up his gun and cracked the door. He heard Laura murmuring quietly and Abby's sleepy voice, but he focused his attention on the outside. He didn't see anything. He didn't hear anything. The birds were singing as though they were the only creatures out and about in the forest.

Seth opened the door only as wide as was needed for his body to slip through. He stepped outside and shut the door, taking time to cover it up as much as possible with foliage. If there was danger out here, he wanted Laura and Abby to be as concealed and safe as possible. Seth walked around the cabin. He saw the footprints from the men last night. They had been close. Too close. Looking at the indentations in the mud just feet away from where they'd been hiding made Seth freeze for a second. Then he forced his body to relax and kept surveilling the area.

They were safe. For now. Well, at least from the men. The smell of smoke was stronger than it had been yesterday.

Seth took care of his business and went back to the cabin, making sure to obscure all of their footprints. He called out softly before opening the door. Laura had seemed both ready and able to fight him yesterday, and he didn't want to catch her by surprise. Laura and Abby were both standing in the middle of the room. Laura had the rifle in one hand, though it was pointed down at the ground. Her other hand was holding Abby's little wrist, as though to keep her from pulling away. He closed the door as soon as he was inside.

Abby saw him and, indeed, began pulling at her mama trying to get to him.

"I think it's okay for now. I didn't see or hear anyone."

At that, Laura let go of Abby and the little girl ran to him and hugged his legs. He bent down to pick her up. "Good morning, Miss Abby."

She put both of her palms on his cheek. Her hands were sticky and Seth wondered if she had been sampling the canned fruit. She smiled at him. "Potty!" She said the word proudly, like she was announcing some great accomplishment. Seth laughed and looked at Laura, who set the gun down and walked over to pull her daughter out of his arms.

"Yes, yes. We're going potty. But remember, we have to be quiet."

Seth went back to the door and opened it, peeking out again. It was still quiet. "I'll go out with you, just in case." They went outside and Laura took Abby into the woods a ways. They came back quickly, Laura looking over her shoulder as she walked.

"Was it okay? Did you see someone?" Seth hadn't, but someone could have snuck up on them. The forest was large and there were too many places to hide.

"No. No, we're fine. Sorry. I'm just feeling especially paranoid this morning."

Seth understood that. He remembered past missions where he'd started seeing the enemy in every shadow. He was feeling that way right now. And this forest had a whole lot of shadows.

SIX

Back inside with the cabin door shut and camouflaged yet again, they ate the breakfast Laura had prepared. Well, the food she found. The mood was definitely lighter than it had been through the night, but Laura was now thinking about the day ahead. She wasn't hungry anymore.

"Seth?" He stopped chewing and looked at her. "What are we going to do? I thought about it last night after I woke up, and our options are all horrible. And limited."

"I thought about it, too. It was all I could think about, really."

"And?"

"And? Well, I'm sure headquarters is missing me by now. I bet they're looking. At least, I hope so. We can either stay here and wait for help to find us or we can try to go through the forest and get to safety."

"Go through the forest? You mean the forest fire, right?" Laura sounded scared to her own ears. Too scared.

"Ideally we go up until we can go around the fire," he said. "Or we hope that they get the fire put out and come up to see if anyone needs help. But I just don't know."

Well, he summed that up. The options sounded limited and terrible, even though he was a law enforcement officer of sorts and even though it was daylight and even though her daughter was smiling and talking happily to herself. And even though *everything*—the options were still options in name only. "So what should we do?"

"I don't like sitting here. For one, we'd have to be still and quiet. And we're well hidden, but there is always a chance they could find us. Then we'd really be trapped. Plus, there's the fire."

Laura breathed in deeply, considering his words. He was…not wrong. Keeping Abby pinned up inside, spending every night terrified to move, waiting on help to find them? Laura thought she would lose her mind the first day, especially when she knew those circumstances were going to stretch out into the unforeseeable future.

Seth was watching her, waiting patiently. She liked that he let her process her thoughts and didn't demand instant answers. "I think waiting here is the worst of the two options."

Seth nodded. "I agree. Every way I thought it through, trying to get down the mountain made the most sense. But this is all going to be on you, and I'm sorry about that."

"What?"

"You know these woods. You know this mountain. I only know the public parts, but you know this part."

He was right. Laura remembered how many times her dad had made her walk their mountain. Map it. Learn it. Come to know it on an almost instinctual level where each tree and rock and call of bird was distinct. She'd hated it. Complained endlessly about it. Been thankful when she had left this mountain and never had to do it again.

And now, here she was, sitting in her dad's shelter and thanking God and her father for all those lessons. Seth was right, she did know the mountain. More important, she knew every way off it. She just needed some information.

"What do you know about the fire?"

"It's on the east side of the mountain. It's wide. Moving slowly up."

Seth gave her all the information she needed because he knew exactly what she was asking. If she had to go through this, at least it was with a park ranger. A man who knew forests and fires.

Laura choked on air as she thought about how thankful she was that she had a park ranger here to help her. Her dad might actually be rolling over in his grave right now. Or, not. Malcolm Grant had understood so much more about the world than Laura had ever given him credit for. He would understand this situation with the same practicality that had helped him survive the Vietnam War and a hostile return to his country.

"We need to get off the east side, then."

"Yeah. You know about the breaks?"

"Oh, yeah. The mountain at its finest when it comes to protecting its own." The mountain was geographically set up so that a fire on one side would not spread laterally around it. There was a large river going down one side and a wall of barren rock cliffs on the other. Basically, the mountain was divided into two halves and a fire on one side would not spread to the other unless it came over the top. That had saved homes and people more than once.

"The fire looked like it was going to spread laterally as far as the breaks and then move up."

"So we can't go down. We can try to cross the river. Or the cliffs. Or we can go up and over, hopefully ahead of the fire."

Seth's eyes were serious, all sense of amusement and joviality completely gone. "That's pretty much the conclusion I came to, too. This is where I need your expertise. Which option is the best?"

Laura really hated that she was the one with the information to make this decision. She was terrified of choosing wrong. "Those men are probably trapped by now, too. Don't you think?"

"They have a helicopter, but they still need to hurry. The fire is spreading, and a helicopter is very noticeable up here, especially with all the firefighters and emergency personnel activated."

"Okay. So that means they need to find us fast and then try to get off, as well."

"That would explain why their boss had them search all night. He must know they are up against a ticking clock."

A burning clock, really, but Laura didn't want to make that distinction. "The cliffs are out. I've tried climbing them a couple of times before, and it was nearly impossible," she said. "And that was with climbing and safety equipment."

"Okay." Seth didn't question her assessment. "So the river, or up and over?"

She wanted to say neither. "I really don't like the idea of the river. It's wide and usually has a nasty pull to it. Plus, it's raging right now."

"It is high. I saw it a couple days ago, and I'm not sure I've seen it that full," he said. "I don't suppose your dad left a raft or boat hiding somewhere, did he?"

Laura's lips quirked. "Not that I know of. I mean, he probably wouldn't have told me anyway for fear I'd go on a joyride."

Seth smiled slightly, too. Laura liked it. "So you think over is the best way?"

Laura hated the weight of this decision. "Maybe. I mean, yes. I do. Except we have those men looking for us, and I bet they are going to be picking the up-and-over route, too. It's the easiest choice, for whatever that's worth, and it's predictable that we'd head that way."

"I agree with you there, too." Seth sighed, long and deep. It was a weary sound. Laura felt a similar drag and they hadn't even started yet.

"I think we should head toward the river but plan to go up," she said. "We'll do the up-and-over path, but if we need to try to cross the river we'll be close enough to attempt it."

"You can do that? Lead us over the mountain, but also close enough to the river to use it as a Plan B?"

Laura thought about his question. There were three lives on the line. This was not the time for false bravado and ego. It was the time to assess. And be honest. "Yeah. I can. It'll be a little zigzaggy, because the river isn't straight. But we should have good cover. Yes. I can do it."

Seth didn't question her more. He nodded his acceptance and stood. "All right. Then we should start out. The faster we get going, the faster we'll reach safety. Do you know if there are any bags or packs in here?"

Thankful to do something other than sit and worry, Laura stood. "Yes, we'll be able to take enough supplies with us to last the trip." If they made it, that was.

* * *

If it weren't for the armed men and the forest fire, this would have been a beautiful walk through the forest. Seth had always liked the woods and had spent much of his childhood exploring them with his family. When he'd been in Afghanistan, he'd almost craved them. Seth had walked out of that rehab center and demanded his dad take him to the forest. Any forest. While his dad waited in the car in the parking lot, Seth had limped into the cluster of trees and just breathed. It was the first time he'd felt like he could breathe since the IED had gone off. The forest in his home state of Oregon was every bit as pretty as the one they were currently walking through.

Even though he'd been released from rehab, Seth still wasn't able to live on his own. His injuries, both physical and mental, required almost constant care. Seth's pride hated being dependent on his family for everything. So, he lashed out at them. Yelled at them, called them names, told them that nothing they did for him was right or good enough. He had hurt the ones who loved him.

Then, he'd been ashamed. So very ashamed

of the man he was to them. The man he had become. Of the months abusing them that he could never take back. When Seth had realized how badly he'd failed his family, he could not stay there with them anymore, so he had fled. To the woods.

And he had been in the woods ever since, it seemed. Sometimes they soothed him. Healed him. Helped him understand where he had gone wrong.

But today's trek wasn't a stroll with God and His beauty. Laura was busy navigating their course. Abby was doing her part by playing the quiet game with admirable determination. And Seth needed to be alert for the men hunting them down. He had to stop reminiscing and start focusing or he would add even more regrets to his list. Regrets so big that the list itself might just disintegrate.

They were moving fairly quietly, and Laura was doing a great job of keeping them out of exposed or open spaces. She was carrying Abby for now, though Seth intended to insist on carrying her later. He already had an argument prepared about how they were in this together, a team.

As two people comfortable in the outdoors, they were managing to move without leaving too much of a trace. There were no broken branches. Since they were hiking through the trees, the ground was covered with a thick layer of pine needles and leaves. Seth looked behind them every once in a while to make sure they weren't leaving obvious tracks.

Seth's stomach churned as he looked more closely. Though adept in the forest, there were still signs of their passing. Three people could not move with any semblance of speed without leaving some trace of their route. But Seth thought that speed was more important than erasing their tracks. Especially since he didn't know where those men were in their search pattern. There was a very real possibility that some of the men were ahead and that he and Laura would walk right into them.

A very real possibility that Seth wasn't going to harp on. Every mission had risks. All you could do was be aware. They were. Laura had apologized earlier for all the zigging and zagging, but she said she wanted to be close to the river and stay in the cover of the trees. She had grasped the possibility of the men being in front of them instead of behind them without Seth ever having to tell her.

Laura Donovan was many things. Stupid was not one of them. No. Watching her walk confidently in these woods, barely making sound, charting a course based on trees and trees and some more trees was the opposite of stupid. It was amazing. Seth was good in the woods. He was considered a skilled tracker. He was the one who went in to find lost hikers. And yet, these woods intimidated even him. They didn't have a map. They didn't even have a compass. They just had Laura.

Of course, they were on Old Man Grant's land still, and no one had ever been here before. At least, no one wearing a park ranger uniform. Seth was walking blind right now, in more ways than one.

When Laura suddenly stopped, Seth looked around in a quick three-sixty. He closed the distance between them and made sure to keep his voice low. "What is it? What's wrong?"

Laura shifted Abby in her arms and turned to look at him. "Nothing. I mean, I don't see or hear anyone. I just don't know where to go from here."

"You're lost?" Seth was more incredulous than upset. Laura moved like she was a part of this land.

"No. I know where we are. We're just out of cover."

Seth looked ahead and saw plenty of trees. "What do you mean?"

"The river is going to turn sharply up here. By almost half a mile. The tree cover doesn't turn. It's a beautiful stretch of open ground that seemed almost magical to me when I was young. It's where my dad would take me to fly a kite."

Seth smiled at the image of Laura as a child flying a kite on this mountain. Then his smile faded as the rest of the picture came into his mind. Laura with a mountain man. And that was it. Had she been happy trapped up here with only a grown man?

"Why do you look sad?" Laura's voice was curious, not accusing.

"I was just picturing you up here and thinking that it must have been very lonely."

"It was just me and my dad. And it was a great childhood." She sounded defensive. That wasn't what he wanted.

"I'm sorry, Laura. I'm really sorry. I don't know why my head is so thick, but I promise I'm working on it. Forgive me?"

Some of the warmth came back, though Seth could feel the distance she was placing between them. "Yeah. I'm sorry. I'm a little sensitive about my dad."

Seth could understand that. Family was family. And Malcolm Grant could not have been all bad if he raised a woman like Laura. Laura looked out ahead of her, and Seth wished he knew the layout of this part of the mountain. He hated that she had all the responsibility for this decision. She shouldn't have to be the only one weighing the risks and fearing making the wrong choice.

"A lot of my defensiveness is because I used to agree with you." She was still looking away, and all Seth could see was Laura's back and Abby's sweet face, looking drowsy and flushed as she rested her head on Laura's shoulder. "My parents died when I was seven. Malcolm Grant was biologically my uncle." Seth felt his eyes widen and was glad Laura wasn't looking at him. For all the gossip about Crazy Old Man Grant, no one ever talked about the fact that Laura was not his biological daughter. "And Malcolm came to get me. I was hurt and scared and alone. I would have gone into foster care without him. You've heard about him—the last thing he wanted was a child. But he came and got me anyway."

Seth heard her sniffle and curled his hands into loose fists to keep from touching her.

Comforting her. "He came and he did his very best. And you know what? It was good enough. More than good enough. I'm a functional, well-loved adult. The homeschooling education he gave me helped me excel. I was a well-loved child. But even though I loved him, and I did, I could not wait to leave this mountain. I just wanted to be normal. He was my teacher and my father and all I could think about was how I wanted more."

Her voice was thick with regret, a tone Seth recognized. One that tugged at him and made his own throat swell with longing for a chance to have done things differently. She sniffed one last time and Seth watched her straighten her shoulders and stand a little taller. Well, taller for her. She turned and looked at him then.

"Sorry. I'm done."

Seth started to tell her she never needed to apologize for her feelings but she shook her head, holding her hand up in a stop gesture. "I can't anymore, Seth. Let's just decide which way we're going."

Seth actually clenched his jaw shut for an instant to keep quiet. He was in no position to insist that anyone talk about their past or regrets. And she wasn't wrong. They needed to keep moving. "I hate to say this again, Laura, but it's your call. I trust you. Which direction do you feel better about taking Abby in? The meadow closer to the river or the trees farther away?"

She looked in two different directions, back and forth. Her hand was rubbing circles on Abby's back again. Slow, repetitive movements that were almost calming to watch. After a very long minute, Laura took a deep breath and pointed to the trees. "I feel better about the trees. If we need to, we can make a run for the river. But, like I said before, crossing the river is going to be hard. The trees at least give us a chance to hide."

That assessment was fair enough. "Okay. I agree. Let's head to the trees."

Laura took a step forward, and Seth reached out to touch her arm. He tried to ignore how nice it felt to make contact with her warm skin. Instead, he gestured to Abby. "You've been carrying her for a long time. Please give me a turn?"

There was no long, tense wait like there had been the first time he'd asked to carry her daughter. Instead, she gestured to his shoulder. "Okay. But only if you let me carry the bigger pack."

Seth wanted to say no. He really wanted to say no. But he'd been raised by a fierce mama and had three older sisters. Yeah, he knew exactly where a *no* would land him in this situation. Instead of answering, he just took off the pack and set it on the ground, reached out his arms and gathered the still-dozing little girl into his arms.

He was shocked again at how light she was. How her little arms wrapped around his neck. How her face nuzzled his shoulder without the slightest care in the world. Abby had abandoned the quiet game for a nap, and she seemed more than happy to use Seth as her mattress.

Seth had nieces and nephews. Several. He'd been deployed when they were born. Then, later, he'd been too broken to enjoy them. What did they look like now? Maybe he even had another one. One who would never know him. That was a small distinction since none of them really knew their uncle Seth.

Abby made a murmuring noise and shifted her head, and Seth realized he had increased the pressure he was using to hold her. He forced himself to relax. This wasn't the time. It was never the time to go down that road.

Laura shouldered the pack and started

walking. She stopped after a few feet, bent over to pick up a large branch and began to use it as a walking stick.

"Have you walked over the mountain before? I mean all the way?"

Laura looked surprised at his question. "Yeah. Several times. It's been a few years, but I still remember." She gave him a goofy grin. Seth really liked that teasing look on her face. "If I'd been able to get school credit for it, I would have a PhD in walking around this mountain."

"All right, then, Doctor Donovan, do you have any idea how long it might take us to go over? To get to the nearest house or ranger station on the other side?"

"It's about fifteen miles until we start to reach civilization on the other side. I'm not exactly sure what we'll find, though, since Dad just stopped us at a certain point. But if he wanted to stop, that had to mean there were people ahead. And people means help."

Seth looked at his watch and considered the distance they had already traveled that day. "If we keep our current pace and don't run into any, um, troubles, it should take us about fifteen hours."

Laura sighed. "I agree. At least fifteen

hours. This is going to be one of the longest days. Ever. And I say that as a woman who was in labor for thirty-one hours."

"Do you think we can walk straight through? It'll be dark before we get over the mountain. Do you think we can walk in the dark or should we camp out somewhere?"

"I think we'll probably need to camp, but can we reevaluate as we get closer?"

"Hey, I'm not in a hurry. It's not like we have reservations or a check-in time to meet."

Laura bit her lip, eyes wide. "The fire?"

Oh, how he wished he had a sure answer to that question. "I don't know. But I think I'd rather hide and rest while it's dark and risk it. At least until the smoke becomes thicker or we see flames."

Their voices were low, hushed. It was probably wiser to be completely silent, but Seth couldn't make himself stop the conversation. He enjoyed talking to Laura. He wanted to know about her.

"Seth?"

"Yeah?"

"What's the plan after we get to safety?"

Seth liked that she was assuming they would make it. Belief in a mission could go a really long way. But she asked a good question. A hard question.

"I don't know, Laura. We need to go to the police. I'm sure they'll protect you. They'll try to catch this guy. But with a forest fire, all resources will be stretched to the limit. Thackery is the closest real town, but it's still pretty small. I just don't know how much they'll be able to do, at least in the immediate future."

Laura didn't argue with him, and that said too much. She knew how small the police force was. And she also had a long history of the police being the enemy.

"Laura, I know I asked you before. But things were crazy then." His lips twitched. "Well, crazier than now. Do you have any idea what's in that safe-deposit box?"

"No." Her voice was a horrible cross between desperate and pleading. "I told you the truth. After Josh died, I moved home. I just boxed up his belongings and brought them with me. But I couldn't go through them."

"But you did eventually?"

"Last week. It's been eighteen months and I finally felt like it was time to fully move on. Deal with the past. I found the key inside a box Josh kept under the dresser. I have no idea what bank it goes to or what is inside."

"Mahoney didn't mention how he knew Josh? Or how he knew you had found the key? It can't be a coincidence that he showed up so soon after you found it. How did he know?"

"I don't know," Laura said. "It's all crazy. Impossible." She bit her lip, looking almost ill. "I keep thinking he must have been watching me somehow. But inside the cabin? Inside my home? That's the place I've always been safest. I just don't know."

"It still doesn't make sense, Laura. Even if they were watching you, they'd have to be really close to see a solitary key. That just seems like too much of a stretch."

Laura gasped. "I called Josh's old firm and asked them if they knew anything about a safe-deposit box."

"You did?"

"After I found the key, I went to town for supplies. I used the cell signal down there to call Josh's old firm to see if they knew about the key. Could Mahoney have been listening to my calls?"

"That sounds more likely than them visually seeing you find a key," Seth said. "What did they say?"

"They said no."

Seth had more questions. But he couldn't think of how to ask them without insinuating Josh had done something wrong—something to bring all this violence to his wife and child.

So he said nothing.

They kept on walking.

SEVEN

Laura was going to get three people killed, including herself, and she would never know why. Even though she was in excellent shape, she was having trouble keeping her breathing even as they walked up the mountain. The air kept catching in her lungs, and she felt like no matter how deep she sucked it in it just wasn't reaching her organs. Laura had never come close to drowning, but this had to be what it felt like. It just had to be.

Laura began moving them away from the river, into where the trees were thicker. The noise was louder in here, too. Or at least it should be. There should be birds and insects and squirrels and the noises from all the animals who lived in these wild woods. But all Laura could hear was her heart pounding.

Her despair was a train, roaring through and blowing its horn. The train really ought to slow down, but it wouldn't. It just gained speed and shot off steam and plowed through whatever might be on the tracks.

She stopped walking. She couldn't move another foot. Not right now.

"Laura?" Seth was there, with Abby, one of his warm hands on her shoulder.

She looked at the ground, afraid to meet his eyes. "Josh did this. Mahoney knew Josh. Knew about the key. Somehow the man I loved did something that is going to get us all killed."

Laura hated the tears running down her face. She wiped them off, trying not to sniffle too loudly. "I'm sorry," she said. "We don't have time for this. I'm sorry." Laura felt calmer just having her fears out in the open. "Okay. I'm done now."

Laura started walking again, away from Seth's warm hand.

"Will you tell me about your husband?" He was walking behind her again.

Laura smiled as a wave of bittersweet memories came over her. She found that she wanted to tell Seth about Josh. She had done a lot of healing in the last few months. "Sure. I left the mountain when I was eighteen. I went to college in Denver and met Josh my freshman year."

Laura flushed, feeling self-conscious at this next part. It made her sound naive. Too simple. But it was the truth, and Laura treasured the way it had all just seemed to happen. "He was the first friend I made. He was my first boyfriend. He proposed our junior year and we married the summer after we graduated. We had Abby two years later. He died eighteen months ago."

Laura's legs were moving on autopilot at this point. Her body was walking through the trees on her mountain but her mind was back in Denver. Back in that time of her life when things spiraled out of control. When nothing she did could make anything better. Her husband had been killed in a freak accident. Her daughter would never know her father, all because Josh was in the wrong place at the wrong time. That was when Laura had realized her dad was right and the outside world was not for people like them.

"My dad came off the mountain to get me. Again. He hadn't left since my parents died, except to buy supplies in town. When I called him, I thought I'd have to leave a message. Wait until he went to town and had a signal.

But he was in town when I called." Laura smiled remembering her shock at hearing her dad's voice over the line. "When I told him that Josh was dead he said he was on his way. To hold on because he was coming. And, you know what, he did. He was there before it got dark, and I didn't have to face a night alone. He held me and told me he loved me and that everything would be okay."

Laura was jerked back into the present when Seth put his hand back on her shoulder. Suddenly, she wasn't in that awful time. No, she was on her mountain. She could hear the birds and smell the pine. And the faint scent of smoke from the fire that was coming up to get them.

"I'm sorry, Laura. You were right about Malcolm being a good man." It was the first time Seth had not called her dad Old Man Grant. "He sounds like a very, very good man. One who was misunderstood."

"He was. He was so gentle, Seth. And hurt. He was just a hurt man doing his very best. Trying so hard."

Seth nodded. "Tell me more about Josh?"

"He was a good man, too. He was. I know it sounds like I married the first man who gave me the time of day, but it wasn't like that. He took the time to get to know my dad. He came up to the mountain and appreciated the world my father had made. He understood that I was the product of how I was raised, and he never tried to change me. When I just wanted to stay home, not socialize, he stayed right home with me. Josh never made me feel weird. Or deficient."

There was a silence and then Seth's voice sounded almost choked. "I'm really glad you found a man like that." Laura wondered what he was feeling to make his tone sound like that. They walked for a bit, the quiet almost soothing after the rawness of her words.

Seth spoke again, his tone causal. "What did you two do for careers after college?"

"Josh was an accountant. He worked at a big firm in Denver. I majored in biology. I worked in a lab until I got pregnant with Abby, and then I stayed home."

"An accountant? Did he ever talk about his clients?"

Laura smiled. "He tried a couple of times, but it was honestly the most boring stuff I'd ever heard. And I say that as a woman who spent years studying single-cell organisms. It wasn't at all exciting or dangerous."

They walked in silence a bit more. Then Seth's voice was hesitant. Timid, almost. "Laura?"

She already knew she wasn't going to like this question. Laura felt the pieces of that brick protein bar she had eaten make themselves known in her stomach. "Yeah?"

"How did Josh die?"

The brick pieces swirled and then sank. Hard. "He was mugged. From what the police said, someone shot him while he was walking from his office to his car in the parking garage. His watch and wallet were stolen." She stopped and swallowed, slow and deliberate, trying desperately to calm the storm in her belly. "And his wedding ring. His wedding ring was also stolen."

"I'm sorry, Laura. I'm really, really sorry."

She had heard that a lot in the days after Josh died. From his coworkers and his friends. From her old coworkers. But from Seth it seemed genuine. And it actually helped a little. "Thank you."

"Thanks for telling me." He sounded sincere. Laura knew he was. It was nice.

Laura felt ready to leave the past behind

and work on the right now. Plus, she needed to focus all her attention on her surroundings. If they were walking into a trap, or a fire, Laura wanted as much notice as possible. Her dad had always stressed the importance of focusing on the task at hand. And she had a major one right now.

She wasn't going to let anyone down.

"I know we're not close to the top," Seth said, "but I can definitely tell we're making progress. The ground is a lot steeper here. I feel like we're walking up a ramp."

Laura appreciated the change of subject. The lifting of mood. She was more than happy to play along with the subject change. Laura smiled at his observation. "Yeah, it's going to stay this steep until we get to the top." She had a sudden mental image of what they must look like, the three of them climbing up a mountain. Fleeing the bad guys. She started to giggle as her mind took the picture and added to it.

"Um, Laura, what's so funny?" He sounded almost scared, like he was afraid she had crossed that thin line between sane and not so much.

"Nothing. I just suddenly realized we probably look a lot like the ending of *The*

Sound of Music. You know, fleeing through the mountains?"

Laura turned to look at Seth and saw that he was also smiling. "Huh. Well, since that movie ended happily, I think I like the comparison. Don't ask me to sing, though."

Seth was smiling and playing along in their conversation about musicals and singing. Abby was still sleeping, and his arms were relaxed as they held her.

Sucking in a deep breath of air, he froze. Smoke. He was definitely smelling smoke stronger than before. He looked up, but could only see blue sky through the tree branches. Laura had done a great job of keeping them in the thicker parts of the mountain, so Seth couldn't see all around. He couldn't even tell which direction the smoke was coming from. He bent down and picked up a dry brown leaf. Letting it drop from above his head, he noted the direction it went as it fell to the ground.

Laura watched him, her expression some kind of grim understanding. It did not do anything to appease the dread building. "You smell it, too, huh?" She sounded like she knew the answer but dreaded hearing it anyway.

"The smoke? Oh, yeah. How long have you been picking it up?"

Laura shrugged. "Not long. I would get the occasional whiff here and there, but the strong hit of smoke didn't start until the last few minutes."

She looked at the ground where his leaf had fallen to blend in with all the others. "The wind is blowing the wrong direction."

He knew what she meant. If the wind was blowing the scent of smoke in, then it was wafting away from the fire, which should be behind them. Straight behind them as they moved up. But the leaf had blown to the side. From where the wall of rock cliff was. "Yeah. That can mean a couple of things."

Seth might not know this mountain like Laura did, but he knew about fires and how they spread. Traveled. Changed and charged and consumed. Destroyed. Killed. "One. Instead of moving up the mountain evenly, the fire has moved up a lot faster on the side bordered by the rock wall."

"And so it is almost racing us up the mountain. And winning."

Yeah, she got it, all right. "Two. There's more than one fire."

Laura's brown eyes darkened, and Seth

knew that she understood him. Her voice was almost toneless when she spoke. "You think those psychos set a fire to try to smoke us out. Or burn us up."

"I know it sounds crazy, but it's actually pretty smart. With the big blaze going, their fire would not be noticeable. People will just think it's part of the original blaze. Plus, it's an efficient way to cover a large search area."

"And by cover, you mean it's a good way to force us out of hiding so they can kill us." Her voice wasn't toneless now.

"Hey, Laura, it's okay. It's going to be okay." Abby stirred as Seth moved closer to her mother, but he didn't stop. Holding the child with one arm, he used the other to reach out and pull Laura into a hug. She came easily, putting her arms around him, sandwiching Abby in the middle. Laura buried her face in Abby's hair, and Seth heard her breathe in deeply. Shakily. Abby's eyes opened. She moved her arms from around Seth's neck and turned to wrap them around her mom.

Laura turned the group hug into her holding Abby. Once she had her daughter, Laura stepped away. Not far, but Seth could no longer feel her body heat. And he no longer had that sweet child against his chest. He found he missed both very much.

Abby was looking at Laura and Laura was murmuring something into Abby's ear. It sounded motherly and warm. Reassuring. Whatever fears Laura had, she set them aside for her daughter. She calmed her child and made her feel safe. Seth wished he had the ability to do that for Laura.

Abby kissed Laura's cheek and said something to her mom. Smiling, Laura kissed the girl back and then set her down on her feet, keeping hold of her hand. "Abby says she wants to walk for a while."

Seth looked at the ground, concerned. Laura smiled, seeming to read his mind. "She'll be fine. She's more than used to exploring the mountain with me."

Seth couldn't stop his smile. "Are you going to lead the way, Miss Abigail?" Seth kept his voice light and teasing, not wanting to undo any of the work that Laura had just done.

"Shhhh. Quiet game." She tried to whisper. Tried, because it was the loudest whisper Seth had ever heard. It made him smile, for real.

Laura's smile looked less real and more worried. The fire. "What should we do, Seth?"

"We know for sure the fire is behind us. It's also coming from the direction of the rock wall. That means the river is still our best Plan B. I say we keep going up the mountain, but maybe stay just a little closer to the river. Just in case."

Laura nodded and started walking. Seth noted that she headed more in the direction of the edge of the trees than she had been before. She was slowly angling them closer to the river. That thing was a beast the last time Seth had seen it. Just a couple of weeks ago. But if it came down to men with guns, a blazing inferno or that river, well, he picked the river.

He really hoped it did not come down to those choices.

Abby was keeping pace with her mom really well. And she wasn't making much noise at all. It seemed all the women in Malcolm Grant's family knew how to handle themselves out in nature. That made sense. For all she might have disliked her dad's hermit ways, Laura had proven to be very much his daughter. She was surely teaching her own daughter the same.

And Seth was beginning to understand the

quiet dignity they all had as a result of this way of life.

They were at the edge of the tree line now. Still under cover, but Seth could see the open meadow Laura had talked about. It was beautiful. He couldn't see the river, or hear it, but he felt reassured knowing that it was there. Just across the open ground.

Just like God is. His heart was hit with the conviction and he missed a step. Laura turned to look at him, and he waved her on. Just as he had God. How many times had Seth assumed that God was not here simply because he could not see Him? Or hear Him.

Seth had been raised in the church. His parents had taught him better. Had shown him better. And still, he had forgotten too many times to count.

But Seth could feel Him now. Seth had come up this mountain, been shot at and was currently trapped by man and nature. If there was ever a time that Seth should have felt completely alone, it was now. But he didn't. He could feel the Lord walking with him. He just knew he, Laura and Abby were not alone in this thing. They just weren't.

The sun was out and shining, and Seth had to squint his eyes. The inner forest had been dark, even though it was the middle of the day. Coming to open ground was shocking in its brightness. His eyes adjusted, and Seth was able to pick up some of the finer details. The small plants growing in the open clearing were blowing slightly in the breeze. The same breeze that was sending one or more fires right at them. There was a sprinkling of color from the scattered flowers that were starting to bloom. The sun was reflecting off—

Seth didn't think, he just reached out and grabbed Laura's arm, the one that was holding Abby's hand. "We have to hide. Now. Quietly."

Laura did not waste time looking around, though Seth knew she must have wanted to see what was making him act like this. Instead, she picked up Abby and put a finger over Abby's lips. Her face was so stern that even Seth felt the urge to shush and stay shushed.

Laura began to walk deeper into the forest, quickly but quietly. Seth followed, turning frequently to look behind him. The trees were enveloping them and any view of that open area and light was gone. But Seth wasn't hiding from grass and light.

Laura stopped and looked at the trees, and

Seth wondered yet again how she was able to know where she was based simply off of a bunch of trees. He was a skilled forester and they all looked the same to him. He could navigate using a compass. Rivers. The stars. But he did not see how one could navigate in a forest full of identical trees.

She turned sharply and it felt like she was backtracking a bit. Seth didn't care, so long as she was taking them somewhere safe. Somewhere hidden. Or at least somewhere that was not here. Seth turned and saw the shine. Again. Except it wasn't a shine. It was a reflection. Sun on something metal. Something that didn't grow on this mountain. And it was heading into the forest. With them.

Someone with a gun was coming their way.

EIGHT

Hide first, figure out what's going on second. Shelter. Then questions. Shelter. Shelter. Laura kept repeating the words in her head, because she really wanted to stop and figure out what they were running from. And how far behind them it was. And if it was going to catch them.

Seth had said *hide* and they had taken off. But she didn't know what they were hiding from. Probably not the fire since you didn't normally hide from fires. That meant men with guns.

Laura had Abby clutched to her chest and was moving as fast as possible without sounding like a woman running through the forest. Thankfully, Abby had picked up on the serious change in mood and was being quiet. When this was over, she was going to let Abby scream and play and giggle for a month solid. While on a sugar high. She certainly deserved it after being so good the last couple of days.

Laura's legs moved from memory, heading to a place she hadn't seen in years. *Please let it still be there. Please.* It should still be there. Her dad wouldn't have destroyed it, but nature itself certainly could have.

Laura turned to make sure Seth was still with her. He was. Of course he was. His presence was reassuring. The look of his face, however, was not. He still seemed worried. Almost afraid. And his gun was in hand, ready to fire. Laura moved a little faster, deciding that making some extra sound would be worth it if she could take that expression off Seth's face. Or at least figure out what it meant.

Laura looked up ahead and almost sobbed out her relief. It was still there. She turned to Seth, only to find he was closer than ever. She naturally slowed as she turned and he stepped up and held her arm. He was urging her forward. Taking the hint without any trouble at all, Laura decided to just get into the cave and explain it to him later.

She went toward the grouping of large rocks covered in moss and vines. The foliage looked tight, grown thick. Laura couldn't see the entrance but it had to be there.

Laura put Abby in Seth's arms, barely slowing down at all. He took her immediately, wrapping both arms around her. He also did not break stride.

Laura thrust her hands right into the overgrowth, pushing in up to her elbows until she felt smooth rocks underneath. She probed in the area where the cave should be. And found it. Bending down, she quickly ripped a seam at the bottom and along one side, creating a kind of flap door. Thankfully, the plant life was not thick enough that she needed to take precious time cutting it with her knife.

She lifted it as little as possible and crawled in. *Oh, God, I'm just not sure I can deal with snakes right now. Or bears. Or spiders. Or anything breathing and moving, really. If You could just make this cave empty of the creepy-crawlies or things that want to eat us, I would really, really appreciate it.*

Laura didn't get her flashlight on before Seth crawled in after her. He still held Abby tight, but he smoothed down the flap she had ripped as much as possible. If the person on the outside wasn't looking, he wouldn't even realize there was a cavern. Hopefully.

Laura turned on the light and slowly scanned the area. It was exactly as she remembered. The rocks were clustered together, almost in a U shape. There was a larger slab of rock on top. She'd always called it a cave, but it wasn't technically. That was just the closest description that fit the enclosure. The vines helped to seal it up and cement the effect of being in a cave.

It was tight for three people, especially since two were adults. But they fit. It was dry. And Laura did not see any animals or creepy-crawlies. Or slitheries. *Thank You, God.*

Seth held out Abby and Laura took her. She curved herself against the back wall of the space, sitting with her legs crossed and cradling Abby on her lap. She leaned down and pressed a kiss in the curve of Abby's neck while holding a finger to her lips. Abby hadn't made a sound, but Laura wanted to remind her to be quiet.

Laura moved her finger and Abby squeezed Duckie in her little arms. Her thumb was in her mouth. Laura had been working on breaking that habit, but she wasn't about to deny her girl any measure of comfort right now.

Seth was crouched down, balanced on the balls of his feet. He had his gun out again.

Laura had not seen him draw it—it certainly wasn't in his hand when he passed Abby back to her. He had to have put it away to take Abby and then immediately pulled it out again. Because the danger was still real and right on top of them.

His hands went over the seams of the flap Laura had made, securing it again. To Laura's eyes, it looked as good as possible. They were very well hidden. If she could just quiet down her breathing a bit, they should not be findable.

Seth reached for the flashlight, turning it off. There was enough light to see, but barely. Hopefully, the vines were thick enough to conceal them. Please, let them be thick enough.

Laura swallowed hard and tried to even the rise and fall of her chest. It felt tight, like she needed to gasp for air. She fought the urge. She was fine. Her daughter was fine. Slowly the thundering in her ears quieted down and she didn't feel like she was huffing and puffing anymore.

Seth was still positioned in front of the flap with his back to Laura and Abby. His body was big and broad, completely filling the entryway. If someone did open that flap, they would only see Seth. And his gun.

Laura still had no clue what they had run from. What they were hiding from. But it had to be one of the armed men. The ones who were hunting them down. Why else would he have acted like that? If it had been the fire or an animal or pretty much anything besides a person, Seth would have talked to her while they fled. No, fleeing in silence had to mean fleeing from a man who wanted to kill them. Or men.

Seth was just staring at the wall of plants. Laura wanted to ask him if he saw anything. Or heard anything. Had they been quick enough? Was the man just coincidentally coming this way or was he actively pursuing them? Was it a man or men? And how many?

The questions flew through Laura's mind faster than she could process them. She had the overwhelming urge to run. To pick up Abby and just run and run and run.

They were going to die. Laura's fight-or-flight response was fully engaged, and the flight response was definitely winning out. Laura did not want to be here anymore.

They were going to die.

No. This was not truth. This was panic

and despair. Laura closed her eyes and buried her nose back in Abby's hair, smelling her sweetness. Abby was warm in her lap. Soft. Warm. Alive. Her greatest gift from God. Laura started counting her blessings. Going through all the ways God had been with her. Reminding herself that He was faithful and steadfast. He did not give her a spirit of fear.

This was okay. This was going to be okay. She was a capable woman. She was Malcolm Grant's daughter. She could and would survive what this world threw at her. This was her mountain, her home. She would be safe here.

Laura opened her eyes and saw Seth's back again. She wasn't alone. He was here. He was strong and he was armed and he would not let anything happen to them.

Laura was overcome by the strength of her gratitude. After Josh had died, Laura had come back to the mountain. To be alone. She had decided that her dad was right and being alone was best. The world and its people was not for her. Right now, though, Laura was beyond glad that she wasn't alone. That she had Seth. Whatever might happen, it wasn't just her and Abby against the world.

Laura's feelings for Seth were all caught up

in the trauma of the past days and the relief that she was not by herself. He was a ranger. She was a widow with a small child. But Seth was here and Laura was extremely happy.

Laura saw Seth's back tense, his arms raising the gun and aiming it at the door. She murmured a reminder to Abby to hush and held her close. And waited.

Then Laura heard it. The leaves were crunching. Loudly. There was the sound of men talking. And the thump of feet on the ground. At first Laura thought she was imagining it, that she wanted to hear something to explain the running and hiding so her mind gave her something. But as it got closer and Seth seemed to get tenser and tenser, Laura knew it wasn't a hallucination. It was all too real.

She wished they had been running from the fire. Or a bear. She could make out the words the men were saying.

"Man, I'm about sick of looking at trees."

Laura did not think those were the men from before. Maybe. She didn't know. What she did know was their dash through the woods had been fast. And messy. Neither she nor Seth had taken the time to cover their tracks. If those men had any experience hunting at all, they could probably pick up the signs of their flight. And follow them to their hiding place.

Seth hadn't thought those men looked like outdoorsmen when he saw them at her dad's cabin. *Please, God, let him be right. Cover our tracks and don't let them find us.*

"Shut it, dude. Complaining isn't doing anything besides making me angry. I'm tired of hearing you complain. I'm tired and my feet hurt and I want a real bed and a real meal. But if I can't have that, then I want you to be quiet."

"Okay, okay. We're done here. Let's move on."

Laura felt her heart lighten.

"No, we're not done here. You heard the boss. There are not a lot of places they can be, but that woman is probably good at hiding in these woods. We have to search it all. He said to look under every rock, and I'm not going back there without following orders. He wants them dead and he wants confirmation that it happened."

And Laura's heart crashed into the ground.

The sounds got louder. The men were doing a lot more walking around and it sounded like branches were either being moved or run into. If they were looking under the foliage and forest growth, those men would find the cave for sure.

One of the men made a loud noise. "Hey, dude. Come here. Do you see this?"

Laura's heart stopped completely.

Seth was definitely going to have cracked teeth when this was all over. If it ended in such a way that he was alive to go see a dentist, that is. Seth had never hoped to visit the dentist before, but he was wishing it now.

These two men were doing a much more thorough search than the previous two had done. Of course, this rock-cave thing was a lot smaller than the cabin. Smaller was harder to find. And it had been so well hidden that even Laura, with her innate forest sense, had struggled to find it. So those were things in favor of them not being found.

But Abby was awake this time. Even though she had been admirably quiet, that could change at any time. From what little Seth knew about children, Abby had been beyond good so far. Probably because of her slight fever. That was bound to change sometime. No one was perfect, and Abby was only getting more exhausted and hungry. And probably sick and tired of this walking through the woods nonsense.

And also, this cave thing was small. Tight. Seth was prepared to fight his way out, but he didn't exactly have a lot of room to maneuver if the men found them. And there was absolutely no place at all to hide if the men just started shooting into the enclosure.

Seth wanted to spring at them. To jump out and get the men before the men found them. It went against everything in Seth's nature to sit and wait. To see if they were found. He had been trained to be proactive, and he was much more comfortable bringing the fight to the opponent.

But he wasn't alone. And the grim reality was that these men were not alone. There had been a lot more than two at the cabin. The others were probably close enough to hear gunfire if it came to that. And they probably had radios. No, Seth needed to sit and wait and pray that the men passed them.

"What is that?" They had found something. Hopefully not a trace of Seth, Laura and Abby.

"I don't know. Some kind of print."

No, God. Please, no. Seth's plea was almost guttural, and his hands wavered as they held the gun.

"Dude, what was that?"

"Some kind of animal. A bear maybe. Do they have bears up here?"

"How should I know? Do I look like Ranger Rick to you?"

"That's hilarious. Do you see any sign of the woman? Or that park ranger?"

"No. All I see are trees and leaves. That's all I've seen for two days."

"I'm so tired of this. Maybe they got away?"

"Nah. Boss is monitoring the radio in the park ranger's truck. There hasn't been any mention of them. No one knows they're missing and no one is looking for them."

Seth felt a jolt at that. He'd been gone for over twenty-four hours. Surely someone had noticed he never came back down the mountain? His boss or coworkers? Had it really come to this? He could disappear and no one would even notice?

"Well, that fire is getting closer. I know boss says he's got it under control, but that thing scares me. I don't know why he had to set it in the first place."

"Yeah, well, it's not your job to know why. Boss said this was the best way to kill the woman. They are trapped by the river and the fires will make them run to us."

"I don't know why we don't just set this entire mountain on fire and be done with it. Then we could get back to where they have restaurants. And cable."

"You know why. She knows about her husband's safe-deposit box. Boss needs to make sure she's dead. And, after the last two days, I think he wants to make it hurt." The man's voice took on a gleeful note. "I hope he wants to make it hurt."

Seth didn't know if he felt or heard Laura's gasp, but when he turned around to look at her she had her hand physically over her mouth as though she was muffling her own voice. He wanted to reach out and comfort her but this was the very definition of not the right time. He turned back to the entry and focused on where the men were. He wanted to have as much notice as possible if they started closing in on the cave's location.

The other man sighed loudly. "Fine. But can I be the one to shoot the park ranger at least?"

"Yeah, dude. If boss agrees, you can shoot the park ranger."

The men's voices faded and the sounds of

their search also lessened. They were moving on, searching somewhere else. *Thank You, God. Thank You.*

Seth lowered his gun, but did not stop his vigil at the entrance. Thoughts were whirling around in his head, but he tried to push them away. First, he needed to be sure that the men were gone. And make sure Laura and Abby were safe. Then he could deal with the implications of the men's conversation.

Seth looked at his watch. He waited five minutes. Ten. At fifteen, his muscles started to relax. Well, not relax. Just lose some of their tension. He still had a really difficult conversation to get through. And then they had to leave the relative safety of this place and continue the journey off this mountain. No, it wasn't time to relax.

He sat back and leaned against the side of the wall. His legs ached in a good way as he stretched them out in front of him as much as the space allowed. He looked at Laura. She was still holding Abby in her lap. Her arms were wrapped around the girl like she wanted to cover her and protect her from the world. Both, at once.

Seth felt like he understood. He was struggling with some conflicting emotions and urges himself. His time overseas had taught him so much. One of those lessons was that it is always better to face the truth head-on than to deny its existence. If something was going to be hard and dangerous and risky, well, it was better to acknowledge that. Wade in the muck and deal with it. Pretending it didn't exist would only lead to ambush and unexpected casualties.

"Laura, are you okay?" It was a dumb question, he knew that. Of course she wasn't okay. He wouldn't exactly say he was okay and it was not his whole world being turned upside down. "I'm sorry. I know you're not."

Laura unwrapped her arms from around Abby. The little girl was sound asleep, and Seth envied her ability to leave the tension of this hiding place. Laura's voice was very quiet, but they were close enough together that Seth could hear her.

"They're going to kill you."

That wasn't what Seth had expected her to say. Not at all. Not even a little bit. "If they find us, they are just going to kill you."

"I heard." He wasn't really dwelling on that part, though.

"I mean, I know they're going to kill me," her voice hitched, but she continued, "and

Abby, too. But I…don't know. I just don't know. They're calling dibs on who gets to kill you. And they are happy that Mahoney is going to make my death horrible. How did this happen?"

Seth didn't know how this had happened. He just knew that it had. And now they had to deal with it. "It's okay, Laura. They're not going to find us. We'll make it off this mountain." Seth prayed that he lived to see the truth of that statement. It hit him that the worst part of being killed was that he wouldn't be there to protect Laura and Abby. He'd never know if they made it out okay.

No. That wasn't going to happen. He needed Laura to keep hope. To believe. She was smart enough to realize if he was telling her to do something he wasn't doing himself. So he needed to do it with her. For her. And for himself. It was one thing to be realistic and practical and aware of the dangers. It was another thing to get caught up in defeatist thinking. Seth wasn't going there. Not today.

They just sat there, held tight in the space that cave made. The men were probably long gone by now, but Seth wasn't in a hurry to leave this safe little place. He wished they could just curl up together, the three of them, and forget what was on the other side of that foliage.

But they had to leave. Their escape path was narrowing. They were scared. And it all just felt very pointless.

"Laura? Do you know what's inside that safe-deposit box? How Josh came to be mixed up with Mahoney?"

She bent her head down, breathing into Abby's hair. Seth hated that he couldn't read her expression, couldn't tell what she was feeling. Besides fear, that was.

"Laura, look at me." He waited until she did. "I know that was a shock. I believe you when you say you don't think Josh was involved with this. I believe you."

He wasn't sure if he did. But she needed her husband to be a good man. And Seth didn't see any advantage to proving her wrong. At least not now.

Laura's voice was distressed. Pleading, as though she automatically expected him to disbelieve her. To call her a liar. Turn against her. "I'm sorry, Seth. But it has to be a mistake. Josh would not have been involved with a criminal."

NINE

Laura owed Seth an explanation. Actually, Josh owed both of them explanations. But he wasn't here and Laura just couldn't believe that he was anything less than the good man she knew. Seth was asking the same questions that were pounding inside her own head, though. Because they both needed to know why they were suffering like this.

And Laura could tell that Seth was trying very hard not to pressure her. To let her sit with the idea that this was all some kind of mistake. She appreciated that.

That is what made Laura try to answer his question. "I know it doesn't make sense. The key was in Josh's things. Mahoney came because of the key. The man is an awful criminal. But there is no way Josh was involved with him. It is just not possible." She held herself very still as she waited for Seth to respond. This was the part where he accused her of being naive and delusional.

"Okay."

Okay? He just said *okay*?

"I believe you, Laura." He leaned back fully and stretched his legs out a bit more. He did not look threatening and his posture was almost comforting. Inviting. "Tell me why you're so sure Josh was not involved."

Even though it seemed Seth was not going to become her adversary, she still felt completely unsettled. Laura took a deep breath and felt Abby slightly trembling in her lap. Regret overflowed in Laura's heart. She had wanted so much for her child. Safety and security. Giggles. Arts and crafts, and pudding and cookies. Friends. Instead, her girl had lost her father. She'd been yanked away from all she knew to live alone on a mountain. And now they were running for their lives. Even though Laura had not told Abby about the danger, the child was well aware that things were bad. And scary.

She began to run her fingers through Abby's hair, smoothing. In theory, the actions were meant to soothe the small girl, who looked confused and scared. It was something Laura often did when Abby was upset.

But it worked both ways. Laura's own breath evened out. Some of the painful stiffness in her shoulders began to melt away.

"First, Josh wouldn't break the law. He was a Christian."

"Christians can mess up, Laura. They can make mistakes." He sounded like he was walking through a house of booby traps and Laura almost felt sorry for him. Except it was her life that was blowing up.

"I know. I know. Josh wasn't perfect. He was as human and fallible as the rest of us. But his faith was strong. He is the one who helped me come to terms with my own faith. He was a good man, Seth."

Seth was just looking at her. Watching. Laura kept moving her hands through Abby's hair. Soothing them both.

Seth nodded slowly. "Okay. In our current situation, it doesn't really matter. There's a safe-deposit box out there that Mahoney wants bad enough to kill three people and set a mountain on fire. That's a good lead we can give to the police."

"If we ever make it to the police."

Seth slid over to where Laura was, angling his body so he was sitting next to her as much as possible in the small area. He took her hand in both of his. Her other hand slid out of Abby's hair and into her lap. Seth squeezed her hand gently and then let go to put his arm around Laura's shoulders. He was holding both her and Abby in a gentle, supportive hug.

The residual tension left Laura's body altogether and she rested all her weight against him. Her head fell back against her shoulder and she turned in to his body, breathing in his warm scent and listening to the steady beating of his heart. Tears welled up and spilled over.

Laura didn't want to cry. Not here, stuck in a literal hole. Not in front of Abby. Not when she felt so weak. But she couldn't stop the tears. It was all too much. She had not been safe out in the real world and she had not been safe back home on the mountain. There was nowhere she was safe. Worse, there was nowhere she could keep her daughter safe. Her daughter was in danger, it was somehow her fault and there was nothing anyone could do.

The only person who had ever been able to make her feel safe was her dad. And he was gone.

She muffled her sobs in Seth's chest and felt him wrap his arms to more completely embrace her and Abby. Abby's little hands patted her on the back and she cried harder that her sweet daughter was comforting her instead of the other way around. When it was over, and she could hear beyond the cries of her own heart, she became aware that Seth was murmuring to Abby.

"Your mommy is fine, honey. She's just feeling sad and sometimes we cry when we're sad. But she is okay. She loves you and everything is going to be okay."

Laura laughed and moved her arms to complete the group hug. She felt better, as though she had bled out some of her pain. "Seth is right, honey. I'm okay. I just got sad for a minute, but I'm okay." Laura lifted her head and looked at Abby, cupping her chin with one hand and stroking her cheek with the other. "Are you okay, baby?"

Abby nodded and hugged her even tighter. Laura looked at Seth. She didn't want to peer in his eyes and see whatever was lurking there, but she owed him that much. But looking made her even more confused. She thought she saw affection. And sympathy.

He should hate her for dragging him into this mess. But he didn't act like he hated her at all. Laura added that to the list of things to figure out once this whole mess was over.

"What do we do, Seth?"

His hand was rubbing her shoulder, and Laura was leaning into it. She had missed the touch of another person, of someone who was not Abby. She had not had physical contact with someone besides Abby since her dad died. It had been months. It suddenly felt like it had been decades.

"Priority one remains getting off this mountain. We keep on with our plan, staying in the trees as much as possible, tracking the river, heading over the mountain."

Laura nodded. So much had happened and yet they were still in the same place. They still had the same objective. The same plan. It was back to her. Her turn to step up and do her part, use her knowledge of this place to get all three of them to safety.

Laura had felt like throwing up when that man had called dibs on killing Seth. And when he talked about her forthcoming painful death. But she couldn't think about those things now. If she let fear cripple her, she might as well walk out there and turn herself in to Mahoney.

"How did you know they were there? I

didn't see a thing." That part had really been bothering her. The first indication she had that something was wrong was when Seth made it clear they needed to get out of there and hide as fast as possible. How was she supposed to lead them to safety if she couldn't even tell when the enemy was close by? She was supposed to be the expert out in these woods. She should know when humans were present, especially since it was such a rare event. Yet, she had not even known for sure what they were running from.

"I saw a reflection. I wasn't positive it was them—I just knew the sun was hitting something metal out there. And I knew metal didn't belong in these woods."

"I didn't see that. I completely missed it."

"Hey, Laura, look at me. No, really look at me." She did. "That's not your fault. You had Abby. You had to map out our path. You had a lot to do. I'm not blaming you. It's not your job to do everything."

"I know." But she should have seen sun reflecting off metal. If she missed that, would she miss a more subtle sign? Would she lead them right to the men? Lead Abby and Seth to their deaths? If that happened, Laura would never forgive herself.

* * *

She said she knew it wasn't her fault, but Seth could see the truth in her eyes. Laura was feeling like a failure. She was blaming herself.

Seth had felt fairly helpless for the last two days. Unable to step up and make it right. But this was something he could try to fix. Something he needed to resolve, right now. "Laura, please listen. Really, really listen."

She looked at him and there was fear in her eyes. That was unacceptable. Completely unacceptable.

"It's not your job to do anything. I know you've been taking the lead on this. That we've needed to rely on you because you have the expertise on this mountain. But you're not alone. And I'm not helpless."

As he spoke, some emotions rose up inside that he hadn't been aware of carrying. Hadn't known were lurking in his heart. A kind of defensiveness. A need to prove that he was a capable man, strong and able to protect them.

He had hurt his family and had run because he could not figure out a way to make things right. He'd felt like a dog with his tail tucked between his legs for a very long time. But he wasn't that. "I'm a grown man who grew up in the Oregon woods. I'm a trained park ranger. I have outdoor skills, too. Hunting and tracking. Navigating in the forest."

She was looking at him, and he saw her throat move as she swallowed.

"You have the knowledge of this mountain, and I am beyond thankful for that. But no one person can do this, Laura. No one person should have to do this. I'm here, and I am more than just another body. I want to help. I need you to let me help."

She was still listening. Still looking at him. Here, in this enclosure, with that sweet child on her lap, Laura looked very small. Very alone. But she wasn't alone right now, and Seth suspected that she had been alone in the past for far too long. He knew all about that.

He'd been alone, too.

And Seth was tired of it. He had a family back home. A family who loved him. Wanted him. And he ran because he couldn't swallow his pride. Accept their help. Avoid taking his anger at his wounds out on them. Laura did not have any of that. They were both suffering from the same thing but Seth's was self-inflicted. He'd known he had made a mistake about a week after he'd left. Then, he had spent more than a year telling himself he needed to live with the choices he made. Now, though, after all this running, of watching this incredible woman, Seth decided that he was going to try to fix his mistakes. If God gave him another chance, he would not take it for granted.

Seth tried to put every ounce of his determination and sincerity into his voice. "You worry about keeping us on course and helping us find a safe place when we need it. I'll worry about whether the fire is catching up or where those men are. We're a team, and that means you can rely on me for some things. In fact, I want you to rely on me. Please."

"Okay." It was whispered, but Seth thought she was perhaps shy instead of hesitant. Something shifted in his soul; something happened in this space. He was more open. Hopefully that shyness on Laura's part meant she picked up on it, too.

But they had to get off this mountain. It was literally on fire. Their escape options were shrinking. And these men were not going to give up anytime soon. That was okay, because Seth was not going to give up, either. And he would put his will up against someone else's any day of the week.

Seth was feeling alive again, the blood

pumping hard through his veins. But this time it wasn't pumping with fear. Nope. This time his body was surging with determination. "So this area was just searched again." His voice was brisk. No nonsense. It was time to set aside emotion and focus on the mission. They needed to get out of this cave. "That probably means it's safe, for now."

"Yeah, but they know the fire is closing us in. They are using it. The search area is getting smaller and smaller."

"You're right. So we need to up our level of caution. And that river is becoming much more viable as a Plan B."

"I really don't want to cross it with Abby."

"Me, either. But if it comes to that, we'll do it. And it will be okay."

"Okay. We have about four hours of daylight left. Traveling in the dark is sounding better and better to me."

"Agreed. So let's go. We'll be careful, but we're going to keep moving. If you know of any more of these hidey-holes, a route that takes us past them might be worth a slight delay."

"You think we're going to run into more men."

Seth paused. But he would not lie to her.

"Yes. I do. But they seem to be completely lost in the woods, and that will definitely work in our favor. They don't seem to know how to track. Or how to move quietly. We'll use that."

Laura breathed in deeply and sighed it out. Seth almost smiled as he watched the slump leave her shoulders. He could practically feel her gathering herself up. She shifted, putting Abby on her feet, and whispered to her. Seth could hear her telling Abby that they were going to go outside again. That they still needed to be as quiet as possible. That it was dangerous, but Seth and Mommy were going to keep her safe from the bad men.

Seth couldn't see Abby's eyes, but he watched Laura look intently into them. Then she smiled and kissed Abby on the forehead. Laura looked at Seth. "Okay. We're ready. Let's go."

Seth lifted the flap up slowly, and peeked outside. He saw nothing unusual. Heard nothing but the normal sounds of the forest. The smell of smoke had become constant, but the sky still looked blue.

He held out a finger to Laura, gesturing for her to wait while he checked it out. He kept his weapon at his side, but was ready to lift it and use it if needed. He lowered the flap, concealing Laura and Abby inside as much as possible. After walking around for a couple of minutes, Seth felt confident that it was as safe as it could be in their current circumstances. He holstered his gun.

He opened the flap and saw relief take over Laura's face. "It's okay. We're clear."

Laura came out, and Seth automatically reached down to carry Abby. She came without hesitation, wrapping her arms around his neck and burying her face in the space between his shoulder and his face.

Laura started to walk ahead of them, but Seth reached out and took her hand. She looked surprised, but she didn't pull away. They moved forward then, a little group of three. Laura was still in the lead. Seth was looking all around, trying to make sure he would see if they ran into the men again.

He knew he was being ridiculous, but he was thankful Laura was going along with it right now. He was going into the territory of hypervigilance. There was a fine line between being aware and getting paranoid. Between observing your surroundings and stressing your body out so much that it began to misfire. Stopped functioning the way it should. Seth forced himself to take it back a step. He squeezed Laura's hand and then let go, wrapping both arms around Abby.

As much as he had liked walking with her warm hand in his, he knew this was better for their safety. He was able to keep up and observe their surroundings a little better. He could watch his footing while holding Abby.

Laura gave him a concerned look, and he just smiled at her. He tried to look reassuring, but was glad he didn't have a mirror to see if it worked or not. It must not have been too bad of an approximation, though, because Laura smiled back and continued leading the way.

She was going a different way than before. They were still in the cover of the trees, but they weren't on the route they'd been on when Seth first saw the shining reflection. He reached out and touched her back. "Why are we headed a different way?" His voice was as soft as he could make it and still have it be audible. He felt bad questioning her, but he wanted to understand where they were going as best he could without actually knowing what the land looked like up here.

"I'm still taking us in the same direction, but I want to incorporate possible hiding

places into our route." Her voice was so soft
that Seth only understood what she was saying by looking at her lips while listening. He
nodded and gave her a thumbs-up sign, and
she started walking again.

For all that being a hermit's daughter had
caused Laura pain in her life, it seemed like it
was the very thing that would save theirs. Her
knowledge of these woods was so complete
that it was almost unbelievable. Even people
who lived on the other side of the mountain
probably didn't know their land as well. It
was one thing to live in a place. It was another thing entirely to have that place be your
whole world. This mountain had been Laura's
whole world for a very, very long time.

The trees thinned out and Seth tried to see
if he could tell where they were on the mountain. There were small patches of snow that
had not melted scattered here and there, indicating that they were making progress in their
goal to go up. Even though it was spring, the
snow would probably get heavier the higher
they went. But snow was good because up
was good.

The heavy canopy over them finally gave
way and Seth found he was ready for blue

sky. A reminder that there was a whole world out there for them. More than tree after tree.

Instead, he saw smoke. Thick, heavy. The entire sky was black.

TEN

This alternate route took them closer to the open fields than Laura would have gone otherwise. But she knew of a couple of hiding places this way and those things had proven to be really, really useful. So she chose this route.

Which meant that she took them right into the fire. In her effort to keep her daughter and Seth safe and alive, Laura had walked them right into the hot spot. Some guide she was turning out to be.

Laura didn't even try to force the shock off her face before turning to look at Seth. She was stunned and scared to her core and there was no way she could pretend otherwise. She simply wasn't that good of an actress. She would have said something, but all words had fled. The phrases had seen that smoke and understood its implications and run far, far away. She and her baby were stuck here, but at least her words were safe.

"I don't smell the smoke, so that's a point in our favor." Seth was not shocked. At least he did not look or sound shocked. Maybe he was better at suppressing his emotions, but Laura didn't see any signs of distress or panic in his demeanor. That was okay because she had enough for both of them.

"The smell of smoke is the same. Constant, but not overpowering. It's coming this way, though. That wall is definitely headed at us." He continued on as though he were talking to a functioning adult.

Abby looked at Laura and she flinched. Her daughter had the same shocked expression on her face that had to be gracing Laura's own. Her daughter was scared. Sick. She should be bundled up on a couch, watching cartoons and eating soup. With medicine.

Not okay. If Seth could focus, look at this newest threat objectively like it was just another obstacle, then Laura could, too. She would. She slowed her breathing. She knew how to handle this. Fires were not uncommon in the Colorado mountains. Her dad had not just taught her about what to do, he had drilled it into her head.

"The animals here aren't alarmed yet. I don't see a flood of them fleeing the blaze."

Seth looked around and slowly nodded. "That's good. That's really good. That smoke looks bad, but we're not in the thick of it." Yet. Laura absolutely heard that little word that Seth did not say out loud. She felt its echo in her soul.

"Yeah. And we don't want to be anywhere near it. The smoke is something else. That blaze has got to be a monster."

"Do you think we can still make it up the mountain? That smoke isn't just coming from the side. It's almost catty-corner in front of us."

Laura looked at the smoke. It seemed alive, and she could almost see it moving. Not just caging them in at their side, but coming at them somewhat head-on. She mentally went up the mountain, seeing the different paths they could take. The river was looking more and more appealing, so Laura concentrated on the routes that ran parallel to it.

Fires were dangerous, and they could move awfully fast in the right circumstances. Laura could conceive of three nightmare scenarios. One, the fire could chase them to the river and catch them before they made it to the water. Two, the fire could circle around them and somehow come between them and the river.

Or three, they would make it to river before the fire got them but then drown or be pummeled to death by the boulders hiding in the current.

Laura's stomach churned as all three scenarios played out in her head. No. No, no, no. This was not going to happen. *Please, God. Give me the wisdom and strength. Help us to get through this storm.*

"I don't know, Seth. I'm afraid it's going to cut us off. I'm really worried that it will circle ahead of us and come down between us and the river. We can't get caught in the middle. We just can't."

Seth shifted Abby to one arm and wrapped the other around her. This was not the time or place, but Laura couldn't stop herself from taking comfort from this strong man. She needed to soak up some of his strength. His confidence. His calm.

"It's okay, Laura. It's going to be okay."

She couldn't help but laugh, even if it was choked up and muffled. "You keep saying that. You've said that at least twenty times in the last two days."

"Because it's true. I have faith." Seth sighed, looking her in the eye. "Or at least I want to. I want to so much. I want faith, Laura. Faith in God. Faith in my abilities. Faith in your abilities." Another sigh, but his voice was still sure. "We are going to be okay." He sounded like he believed it. Very convincing. And it helped. Hearing his firm belief that they could overcome any obstacle they encountered, including fires and guns and mysterious bosses, helped her to believe it, too.

He squeezed her then, increasing the pressure in such a gentle way that he was almost physically holding her together until she was ready to take over the job. He had a Donovan woman in each arm, and he still seemed strong enough to take on the rest of this mess. Laura had missed knowing someone else was there. Having someone she could lean on.

She had missed having a partner.

After taking a few selfish moments, and thanking the Lord that she was able to do so, Laura straightened and stepped away. She bent forward and put a hand on each of Abby's cheeks, leaning in to kiss the little girl's forehead, eyelids, nose and chin noisily. Abby laughed and Laura found it impossible to be scared when her daughter was giving off such joy.

Laura let go and looked at Seth. "Okay, I'm ready. I think staying within eyesight of the river should be priority number one. I'll feel a lot better if we can see our Plan B at all times and know it is still there and viable."

Seth didn't hesitate. "Sounds good to me."

"That means we're giving up some cover. And we're giving up access to some hiding places I know."

Seth nodded. "I get it. I'm with you that the river is the most important, though. We'll be as careful as possible, but we need to get off this mountain. Now."

The words weren't even fully out of his mouth before Laura started walking. There was nothing worse than standing around feeling uncertain. Anxious. Laura was ready to move in the right direction.

Her pace was faster than before, though she was still sure to not break branches or leave a very noticeable trail. She headed directly to the river, and some of the instinct to run lessened when she heard it. It sounded fierce. This time of year was when the river was at its fullest. The snowmelt swelled the rivers and they came crashing down the mountain, wearing down rock and anything else in their path.

It was a white-water rafter's extreme dream. And one of her worst nightmares. If they had to get in that water, then things were bad.

She stopped her direct path to the river and began moving back up the mountain, this time angling until the water came into view. The final bit of instinct telling her to run for the water died down then. She could see it. Plan B was as safe and as viable as a crazy Plan B could get.

She turned to make sure Seth and Abby were still with her, and of course they were. Just like before. They were right there and they were safe and she was safe and she was not alone. Her looking had less to do with wanting to make sure Seth was doing what he said and more to do with the way seeing him reassured her.

Abby was staring at the river, obviously enthralled by the rushing water and the loud roaring sound it made. She was pointing and saying something to Seth, but the sound of the river drowned it out. Laura could only see her daughter's smile. And Seth's gentle one in return.

Josh had died when Abby was just a baby,

but Laura imagined that he might have looked
like that holding his daughter. She felt the familiar pain that came when she thought about
her husband, but it wasn't crippling anymore.
She still had no clue how Josh was involved
with Mahoney, but her husband had been a
very good man. He would have been an excellent father. But he wasn't here. Laura liked
to think that he was in Heaven, watching her.
And she knew that he would not want his wife
and daughter to spend the rest of their lives
mourning him. He would want them to find
happiness again.

Laura had thought happiness meant safety
up on the mountain. Now she wondered about
her plan. About the full life she might be de-
nying Abigail. Mountain life had been the
best her father could do, but Laura knew the
man had settled for as much peace as he could
find. He'd encouraged her to leave, to go to
school. To start her family out in the world.
Malcolm Grant had wanted a full life for her.

Laura's foot caught on a rock and she jolted
back to reality. She had no idea where all
these thoughts were coming from, but this
was not the time. She could not afford to
make a mistake because she was lost in her

own head. Laura pushed those thoughts inside a box. She would take them out later.

She smiled. So far she had scheduled a nervous breakdown and an examination of how she felt about her dead husband for later. For when they were out of this situation. When she and Abby got to safety, Laura was going to be very, very busy. She was almost looking forward to it.

Abby thought the river was pretty. And loud. And pretty loud. Seth knew this because the little girl had told him. Several times. While pointing. Seth was grateful that the river was loud enough to cover her voice because the last thing Seth wanted to do was hush her, especially after she had been so good during the whole thing.

He'd seen Laura stumble a bit, but she regained her stride without any help from him. He'd been watching the expression on her face and her furrowed brow and had wondered what she was thinking about right before the rock caught her toe. Whatever it was, she had either stopped thinking about it or she was doing a better job of hiding her emotions.

Seth looked at the wall of smoke in the distance, then at the river that was almost startling in its strength. Violence. And then Seth saw a couple of blooming wildflowers against some large boulders. This would have been an amazing and beautiful picture. The kind of thing that made viewers wonder if it was Photoshopped or made up. In reality, though, standing between two of nature's deadly and powerful forces, knowing there were several armed men out there trying to kill them, it lost some of its appeal.

Laura started leading again, moving at a pace that impressed Seth. They'd been walking for hours, yet she was willing to carry on at the necessary pace. All without complaint. She managed to do it gracefully and without disturbing the ground she covered. He kept up easily, but he could feel his blood pumping from the activity. It seemed Laura had decided that speed was just as important as stealth, and looking at the black wall in the sky in the distance Seth agreed wholeheartedly.

She brought them back under the cover of some trees, and Seth relaxed a fraction. He could still see the river, and Seth wondered how long the cover lasted if they stuck to the strategy to stay in sight of Plan B. He wasn't going to ask, though. He didn't want to distract Laura. He didn't want to make any extra noise. And, truly, part of Seth did not want to know the answer to that question because he was guessing they would not have near as much cover as they needed.

It was a beautiful day, and they seemed to be making good time. The snow went from a splotch here and a splotch there to bigger patches. Seth could see large covered areas in the distance. The air was cooling down, but he didn't feel cold. Abby was dressed in layers and she did not seem to be cold, either.

The silence was peaceful and they walked in such a way that his feet were almost making rhythmic motions. All of it was soothing. The atmosphere felt almost like a prayer, that mood of contemplative quiet. Seth had not felt that atmosphere in a long time. Too long.

He was almost unnerved by it. Yes, he was keeping watch. He was vigilant and well aware that danger quite literally surrounded them. But he was also full of emotion right now. Feeling. It was like he was climbing up to God, and the higher he got, the more he shed the distractions of this world, and the better God was able to communicate with him.

That was a silly notion. God could communicate with him anywhere. Under any circumstances. Yes, the Lord was always present and speaking to him. The problem was, Seth did not always listen. He was able to fill his life with noise and distractions and tasks. He was able to avoid that still quiet voice in his soul. That nudging of his conscience. The gentle prodding of the One who knew all.

But it was almost impossible to ignore up here. Seth felt it flooding over him as strongly as the waters in that river would if they were forced to try to cross it. He smiled when he realized how fanciful his thoughts were. Ridiculous. Maybe they were farther up this mountain than he thought and the high altitude was getting to his brain. He was daydreaming like a child. Seeing what he wanted to see.

"Are you okay?" Laura's voice was hesitant. Almost with a hint of fear. That softened Seth's natural instinct to deny anything was wrong. Or resent her noticing that something was off. He wanted to be real with her. He did not, however, want to analyze that desire too much. This wasn't the time or place for thinking soft thoughts about this woman. They had a job to do.

"Yeah. Sorry. I was just thinking."

They were still moving at a decent pace, still under the light cover of trees. He shifted closer to her so that they could talk without raising their voices, though the roar of the river carried this far and helped to mask much of the sound.

"You looked like you were in pain."

Seth smiled. That was certainly one way to describe it. Thinking about how God had to get him on a mountain between a forest fire, a raging river and armed men with homicidal tendencies before Seth would listen to Him was kind of a painful realization. "I was just ruminating."

"It's kind of hard not to up here, isn't it?"

"That's probably understating it. My brain was just racing."

"Want to share?" The words left Laura's mouth and then she quickly turned and gave him a wide-eyed look. "I'm sorry. I'm not trying to pry." Her words were coming so quickly together that Seth felt like he was hearing her about two seconds after they left her mouth. "I just mean, you know so much of my messed-up life. You listened while I told you everything. I just thought, I mean, maybe, I don't know. If you want to talk, I'm here. If you want. I mean, you don't have to."

She sounded so sincere and afraid of upsetting him. It was such a sweet and beautiful thing. She should be focused solely on getting herself and her daughter to safety. But instead, she was finding the time to care about him. To worry about him.

Well, why not? Wasn't his desire to do everything himself what had gotten him in this mess to begin with? Not the mess of running from armed bad guys, but the mess of being away from his family. Being alone, even though he was in a world full of people.

"I was just contemplating how hard it is to avoid thinking up here. It's so open and quiet that a lot of the thoughts I had shoved away were coming back."

"About your time in the military?"

Seth stopped to look at her. "How did you know that?"

Laura's smile was almost rueful. "I recognized the look. You know a lot about my dad, but did you know that he was a Vietnam vet?"

"No. I had never heard that."

"Yeah. He had a hard time over there, from what I know of it. He came back and that's when he became, well, isolated. The hermit thing didn't start until he came back. I can remember my biological dad explaining it to me once. They were brothers. I remember asking why Uncle Malcolm was so weird and scary and my dad telling me it was the only way he found to keep living in this world after the war."

"And I remind you of him in that way?" Seth wasn't exactly insulted. There was a lot of truth in the comparison. For someone who used to make fun of the man, Seth was realizing much of Old Man Grant could be found in his own mirror.

"Just a bit. You come off like someone who served in the military. Who knows war."

"I did. I do. I did three tours in Afghanistan. Got hurt. Came back."

That was the very abbreviated version, but Laura just nodded and started walking again. Her manner was easy. All encompassing. She was good at accepting what a person could give. And Seth found that he wanted to give more. To her, at least. He suspected that she knew a lot about regrets. About being judged. About acting without knowing how or why.

"My family tried to help me. Nursed me back to health. Took care of me." His voice was rough and his chest was so tight that he thought it might split in two. How could talking about that time hurt worse than war?

Laura kept walking at a steady pace. And that made it better. Not seeing her face. Not seeing her eyes. That helped.

And he was all the more a coward for it, but he accepted it gratefully.

"I hated it. I hated that I was a grown man who needed his mommy to take care of him. I hated the way all my friends and family looked at me with pity in their eyes. Like I was some kind of sympathy case. It was my ego. I know that. Now. It was all pride and ego and anger from feeling helpless."

"That seems like a very rational response to what you went through. Very human. Normal even." Laura's voice was soft, and she was still walking without looking at him.

"Yeah. Maybe."

They walked for another couple of minutes in silence. The words just kept building up inside Seth. He wanted to keep them in, but they wanted out. And really, maybe saying them out loud to someone would help. He'd certainly said them to himself enough times.

"I ran away. I couldn't take it anymore and I ran away. I was a grown man, but I left a note and got in my car and fled."

Silence. What was she thinking? Was she shocked? Disgusted?

"I understand that."

"You do?"

"Yeah. Things were hard after Josh died. A lot of pitying glances my way, too. So I came home. I phrased it like that. Coming home. But it was running away and hiding in the most isolated spot I could think of."

Seth thought there was a difference between her coming home and his hurting his family by running from them, but he didn't want to argue the point.

"They know I'm okay. I write them about once a month, to let them know. I don't include a return address, which is cowardly, but I just can't. I've asked them to give me this time, and so far they have. Still, I know I hurt them." He was still hurting them. There was no way his mother was not hurt every single day that went by without him calling. But, as more time passed, it just seemed like his mistake grew and grew and now it was so big that Seth didn't know if it was fixable.

Laura stopped, turned around to face him. Seth braced for whatever he might see on her face. He didn't know which would be worse, blame or sympathy. Instead, she looked alarmed.

"Seth. Look behind us."

He whirled around so quickly that Abby startled in his arms.

Black. Everywhere he looked was a wall of thick, black smoke.

ELEVEN

It had reached them too quickly. There had not been any sense of fire and now there was a blaze so intense it made the sky look like the dirtiest of nights behind them? No. That wasn't how forest fires worked. At least not naturally spreading ones. Not in these conditions.

"That's not the original blaze, is it?"

Seth's face was as dark as the air around them. "No. Not with these winds. It wouldn't have come up on us like that."

Yeah. She knew that, but she had really, really hoped he would say something different.

Seth did a slow full circle where he was standing, taking in all their options. Or lack thereof. Laura had thought she felt trapped since this whole thing began, but, looking at the current situation, she knew that had been a false perception. Now. Now she felt trapped.

"Seth?"

"They set that fire to chase us out. We have smoke on two sides and the river on a third."

"They're forcing us to go one direction."

"Yeah. And I bet they're up there waiting for us to walk right into their little trap."

Little trap? Right now it felt very large and very, very dangerous.

"What do we do?"

They both looked at the river. It was still raging. In fact, it seemed as upset as Laura felt. "We stick close to the river. But I'm not liking our odds any more now than I did a while ago."

Laura nodded. "Agreed. I really, really don't want to take Abby through there."

"Okay, let's keep moving forward. We just need to be as alert as possible. It's no longer a matter of if we run into the men, but when."

They walked. Slower. Quietly. Every hair on Laura's body stood on alert and her mind was buzzing. After several minutes, she almost wished they would just see the men already. The anticipation was almost too much to take.

"Laura."

They were walking close to one another

now, almost as a single unit, and Seth's low voice carried to her perfectly.

"Yeah?"

"I have two favors to ask of you. I'm sorry, but I have to ask."

"What?" Favors? What exactly could she do for him? Especially now?

"If we run into the men, I'm going to fight them as best as I can. I need you to take Abby and run, okay? Through the river or wherever you think is the safest. But let me do that. Let me fight and distract and buy you some time. Please?"

That was a favor for him? It seemed like a favor for her. But Laura knew why he was asking. The thought of leaving Seth to a near-certain death hit her harder than she would ever have imagined. He was a park ranger. Rangers harassing her dad were the prominent theme of her childhood. They were not her friends.

But she did not want him to die.

Laura looked at Abby. Forced her throat to swallow. "Okay. I'll try, Seth." She hoped that was good enough.

Seth just looked at her, his face almost still. Probing. "The second favor is a bigger one. And it is very dependent on you doing the first. When you get out of this, I want you to get a message to my family. Their contact information is on file with the ranger service. Will you please tell them that I'm sorry and that I love them?"

Laura couldn't breathe. She had to stop walking, and Seth stopped right beside her. She felt his hand on her back, but the world around her was a blur. This man planned on dying. He fully expected to run into those men and to not walk away from the encounter.

That was not exactly shocking considering the odds they were facing. They were on a burning mountain and up against more men than Laura could count. All heavily armed.

Foreseeable or not, though, it still burned Laura's lungs.

And he expected her to survive? He thought, he really, really thought that she and Abby would get off this mountain alive and could get a message to his family? How? How could she pull that off? Laura intended to fight for her daughter until she had nothing left to give, but, deep inside, in the part of her that she hadn't wanted to acknowledge, Laura had fully expected to fail.

That was what turned the hot coals into a

blaze in her lungs. She and her daughter were going to die. She hadn't even known that was inside her. That horrible ending that seemed almost unavoidable.

Except Seth really thought she could avoid it. He was earnest in his request. They were not empty words. He thought she could fix things with his family.

He trusted her to make things right. To help repair the relationships he valued the most.

Okay, then. Her voice was thick, but she put every ounce of determination she could muster into it. "Yes, Seth. Yes. If you can't tell your family, then I will. I'll tell them everything, including what an amazing man they created and sent out into the world."

Seth nodded, squeezed her shoulder and started walking. Laura moved, too.

She didn't know what else to say, but that was okay. Because sometimes you didn't have to say anything. Sometimes, you just understood. Her dad had taught her that.

The river curved up ahead, and they both slowed down. They did not want to round a corner and walk into the ambush that had to be waiting for them. Laura tapped Seth on the arm and started moving away from the river.

She wanted to stay close to good old Plan B, but they also needed some kind of cover.

They entered the trees, which made them less visible. What if the men were waiting in the trees? That was the obvious place for people trying to hide to be.

No. Laura needed to stop this. She said a quick prayer. There. Laura truly believed that worrying about something you prayed over was pointless. She wanted to pray, give it to God and let Him deal with it.

But, oh, it was so hard. And she often failed at the giving it to God and letting go part.

Yeah, she failed at that a lot.

But she always kept trying. That was the only thing she could do. Try and try and try.

Blowing out a deep breath, Laura looked at Seth. He was watching her with an almost tender expression on his face. Her face grew hot and she shrugged her shoulders at him. He smiled back and nodded.

He got it.

And that was nice. Josh had always accepted her quirks with an easy understanding. That had been a precious thing in her life. Laura had assumed she would never have that again.

Maybe she was wrong.

They moved around the curve. Laura was holding her breath, fighting the urge to just run and see. If you thought there was a monster in the closet, waiting in bed and imagining it wasn't the answer.

No. Every child knew that you jumped out of bed and flung that door open.

And Laura really wanted someone to open this closet door. And turn on the light.

But the monsters in the closet weren't real and these men absolutely were. She would not put their lives in danger in the long term because it might make her feel better in the short term.

Seth's hand suddenly shot out and grabbed her arm. Pulled her to a stop. He never said a word, but his message was clear. There was something up ahead. Something bad.

Seth silently passed Abby to Laura, and she squeezed her girl. He moved to walk in front of Laura. They seemed to be creeping, not going forward at all.

But they had to be because they rounded the corner and saw it.

It was a trap.

And that trap was about to be sprung.

Seth led them to a group of boulders that formed a low wall. She set Abby down, and held her finger to her lips. The child had surely picked up on the tension in the air, but it wouldn't hurt to reinforce the need for silence.

Seth and Laura both peered over the little wall, and Laura could not stop her gasp. Thankfully, it was not loud. And the men were far enough away to not hear.

And they were not even looking.

It was amazing, really. For men who had gone to such great lengths to find Seth and Laura, they were almost lounging. Relaxing.

Laura saw seven or eight men. All armed. With multiple guns.

There were several Jeeps with boxes in the back.

The men were leaning against one of the Jeeps, laughing and talking.

Laura rested her forehead against the boulder and felt Seth's hand on the back of her head. She breathed in, trying to find the scent of this mountain she loved under the ever-present odor of smoke. This close to the boulder, Laura could almost imagine she was a child again, alone on her mountain.

Laura lifted her head back up. It was what it was, so she needed to deal. And Laura had a lifetime of experience at dealing with whatever was thrown at her.

She started on the left side of the camp and began to scan to the right, slowly looking and trying to see something, anything, that might help them.

She made it to the far right, and was about to give up, when she froze. How had she not noticed that right away?

"I'm hallucinating, right? This whole thing has finally gotten to me and now I've lost all touch with reality." Laura's voice was the lowest murmur, but she wasn't asking a question. It was more like she was muttering to herself.

"If you're talking about the small army of armed men standing right there, then no. You're not hallucinating."

Laura didn't look at him. She was still staring straight ahead like she had been hypnotized into some kind of trance. "No. Not that."

Seth looked at her profile, but she was dead serious. "No, you're not talking about all those men with guns?"

"No. Look, Seth." She sounded disappointed that he hadn't caught on yet.

He looked. Lots of men, too many to fight. Check. Guns, probably loaded with lots of bullets. Check. Laura reached out and gripped his arm. Not held. Not even pushed or pulled. No, she placed her hand on his forearm and dug her fingers in like she was clinging for all she was worth. She was still staring straight ahead and Seth was moving from confused to some combination of irritated and frightened. What was going on?

"Rafts, Seth. Look. By the river. Do you see a bunch of rafts, or am I just seeing what I want to see?"

Seth had been focused almost solely on the men themselves. They were the threat in his view and he hadn't really taken his eyes off them. Now, though, he scanned the surrounding area. And felt his heart jump. She was right. There. Just over there. Rafts. Three of them. They looked like the kind you would go white-water rafting in for fun or recreation.

"Yes." He had to keep his voice calm and low. The last thing they needed was for the men to find them or for Abby to react to their excitement. "Yes, Laura. Those are rafts."

"I, I, I… What does this mean? Why do they have rafts?"

"This Mahoney is determined. He's prepared. If you're going to bring a small army to a mountain to kill one woman and one small child, you might as well make sure you have enough equipment for any contingency." It made sense in a sick kind of way.

"I want one of those rafts, Seth. How do we make that happen?" Laura's voice was pure determination. Seth had not ever heard her so focused. So intent.

"You think we can go down the river in one? We don't have life jackets or other safety equipment. Even if we made it over there, by the time we get a raft we will not have any time to do more than jump in and hang on." And they had Abby. Seth didn't say that last part out loud because no one needed to tell Laura that they had her daughter with them. She knew. She always knew.

"I can do it." Again, her voice was absolute. It seemed that Laura was going to use the sheer force of her will to make this happen. And from where Seth was crouched down behind a fallen tree, that will seemed absolute. He felt a military battle yell rising up in his chest. Oh, yeah. They were going to make this happen.

"Okay, then. Let's make a plan." Seth started counting men. There were eight that he saw. They were all clustered, almost loafing around. Of course, there wasn't much

reason for them to be up and actively searching. They had done a masterful job of forcing Seth and Laura to come to them. Right
to this camp of horrors.

The good news was that the men clearly
did not know that Laura and Seth were there
already. They must have moved faster than
the men had planned for. Good. Real good.

"All I can think about is grabbing one of
those rafts. They're calling to me like a hom-
ing beacon." Seth smiled, even if it did feel
a bit grim. Zombie Laura was gone and his
wonderful capable Laura was back. They had
proven to be fairly unstoppable when practical and capable Laura was around.

"We need some distraction. Something big
enough and far enough away to get all those
men to run to it. We don't need much. Just
enough time to get to the rafts, throw one in
the water and jump in. Even if they follow us,
it will be near impossible for one raft to catch
up with another successfully in these rapids."

"Do you still have your knife?"

"I— Yes. Why?" She had sounded a little
bloodthirsty when she asked and Seth was
momentarily afraid that she was going to try
to engage in hand-to-hand combat with these

guys. When it came to protecting Abby, Seth wasn't sure he would put it past her.

"I'm going to stab the other two rafts. Deflate them. They won't be able to follow us."

Seth nodded his head slowly as he surveyed the area again. "They still have those Jeeps. They could drive alongside the river, catch up that way."

"Until they hit that fire they set. Can't drive through that." Laura sounded almost smug and Seth smiled. She was right. Again. He handed her his knife.

"They can also shoot at us. The river will move us quickly, but bullets are fast, too. They could hit us. Or the raft. Both would be the end of our escape."

"This is outside my area of expertise. Any ideas how we get past bullets?"

Seth pulled out his gun. "I can try returning fire, but it's me against eight men."

"So, what do we do?"

There really wasn't a choice. They'd been backed into hard positions since this thing first started, but this was by far the hardest. The tightest corner. But it was the corner they were in and they had to just deal. "We try. We pray. We do our best and hope that it works."

"Okay." Laura's voice was not hesitant or

unsure. Seth was so incredibly grateful that he was not alone in this mess. That he had her there with him to help him through. "So what kind of distraction are we going to do? I'm afraid I won't be any help with that one unless it involves me running and screaming. But I don't think that will get us what we want."

Seth smiled. No, that was not going to be the plan. "I don't know, yet. There are some crates and boxes over there. See them? I kind of want to check them out."

"What do you think is in there?"

"I don't know for sure, but I'm hoping weapons. Or maybe even something I could use for an explosion."

"An explosion? You can do that?"

Seth gave her a mock serious look. "Yes, ma'am. I can be real handy with explosions when I need to be." He'd used them more than once in Afghanistan. It had been a couple of years, but those skills were the kind that stayed with you for forever. Sometimes Seth had considered that to be a curse. Right now, though, he was viewing it as an asset to be grateful for.

Seth looked at their current location. "Do you think you and Abby will be safe here while I go check things out? Rig some kind of diversion?"

Laura looked behind her to the grouping of trees they'd been in before almost walking into this trap. "I think so. We might have more cover back there, but we'd have to actually walk that way. I feel safer here without moving."

"Yeah. We were fortunate walking in. Movement could catch their attention. Okay. You stay here with Abby. Be ready to go. I don't know how much lead time I can give us before whatever diversion I come up with, so we might have to move quickly."

Seth started to crawl away, not wanting to dwell on the fact that he was about to separate himself from Laura and Abby for the first time since this whole thing started. He was leaving them. Alone. If something happened, he would not be there to protect them. No, he needed to get on with it. Put their plan into action. It was the only way to get this done. If he lingered too long, thought too much, he probably wouldn't leave at all. Fear could be paralyzing, and the best way was for him to break on through. So he started to go.

But Laura reached out and grabbed his hand. Her grip was firm and her other hand came around so that his hand was clutched between both of hers. "I, um, you're leaving. You're going to leave."

He brought his other hand and added it to the pile so it was a mass of hands gripping and clinging. "It's okay, Laura. I'll be okay. I know how to move without being seen. This isn't the first enemy camp I've explored, though I wouldn't mind if it was my last." He smiled at her, trying to reassure her that this was not the end of the world. He might have a boulder in the bottom of his stomach right now, but he didn't want her feeling that way. Not now, not ever.

She blew out a shaky breath and her eyes still looked distressed but she stopped clutching him in that desperate manner. "You're right. I'm sorry." Laura looked at Abby, who was watching all of this with wide eyes. She reached over and pulled the girl into her lap, snuggling her neck. "I'm sorry. We're good. You go save the day and we'll be ready to run like crazy."

He didn't believe that she was good. But there wasn't anything he could do right now. The best thing for them was to get off the mountain. To get to safety. That was the goal Seth needed to focus on.

He turned from them then. Looking away from these two people who had come to mean so much to him. And he faced the camp. The men lounging around, large guns in their hands. Their barricade. Pushing everything out of his mind, Seth began to make his way to those boxes.

He was a soldier on a mission.

TWELVE

He was gone.

Seth was gone.

Laura had watched him as he moved away. He'd looked like he was going to make a wide circle around the camp, trying to get to those boxes by staying as far away as possible. Laura could not see him anymore. She kept looking at that grouping of boxes, forcing herself to breathe in and out as she waited to see Seth there. Exploring them, as he put it. But so far, she only saw those men with large guns who were waiting to kill them.

No. Getting caught by those men would be the end. Done.

Laura gripped the handle of the knife tightly, squeezing it almost like a pressure ball. She still had the rifle right next to her. Loaded. Ready. But using it would alert every man in this camp that she was here. If she was discovered by one man, she had a fighting chance of protecting herself and her daughter with the knife without bringing the rest of the men running.

The thought of what she was planning made her sick. It was almost too much. She had come to the mountain to be alone. To find peace and safety. And now she was contemplating how she could use a knife to hurt someone.

No. Not to hurt someone. To protect someone. To protect her Abby.

Laura moved Abby off her lap. She had quietly explained to the little girl that they were waiting for Seth and then they were going to run as fast as they could to the raft. Abby had been in boats before, but she had never been white-water rafting. She'd never even seen someone do it.

Laura had explained about holding on. About lying down on the floor of the raft. About staying right by her mommy so she could be safe. Abby had repeated the instructions back to Laura. Hopefully it would be enough.

Laura took her eyes off those boxes to scan the area again. It was the same. Too many men and too many guns. She looked behind her, and her fear ratcheted up another notch. The smoke was definitely closer. The fire the men had set behind them was working exactly as planned. It would eventually force them into the camp.

Laura wondered where Mahoney was. It seemed that the men had plans to get to safety by driving over the top of the mountains in the Jeeps. Or maybe rafting down the mountain. Laura still couldn't believe that there were rafts here. She supposed she ought to be grateful that they were the well-prepared type.

But would they be prepared with the things Seth needed? He was going around in a wide circle to reach those boxes. But there was no way they could make it to the rafts or the Jeeps without being spotted. And given how close the fire was, Laura hadn't even suggested trying to sneak past the men and keep on moving.

This entire plan hinged on some kind of distraction. Away from the river. That was their only hope of reaching a raft and getting down the river in it.

Laura looked back to the boxes and gasped. Seth was there. He had a second knife out and was prying the lid off one. There were three men about fifty feet away. They were not facing Seth, and they were engaged in loud conversation. They were laughing. Happy. Laura felt sour disgust on her tongue as she watched the men who were waiting to kill them laugh and be merry.

She looked back to Seth and held her breath as he lifted the lid. He was moving slowly, and Laura prayed that he was able to be quiet as he dealt with the contents of the box. Laura saw him look inside. She couldn't read his expression.

Seth reached inside the box and began pulling things out, but Laura did not know what they were. Did he have what he needed or was going to try to make do? Laura understood why she and Abby stayed where they were. It was easier for Seth to move around and not be detected. Laura and Abby were currently in the best location to make a dash for those rafts. Even so, Laura found herself wishing she was with Seth right now. Good or bad, she wanted to face the contents of those boxes together.

Seth filled his bag with the mysterious objects and then faded into nothing again. One minute he was in front of her and the next he was gone. *Please, God, be with him. Help him. Make this work.*

Laura quickly went through the pack and took out things she thought they could live without. It was heavy and would slow down their run to the rafts. She kept some food. Some basic first-aid supplies. Taking Abby's duck from her, she explained that Duckie was going to ride in the bag. It seemed silly, but odds were good that the cabin had been consumed by the fire. That duck might be the only thing her sweet girl had left, and she deserved to take her only friend with her.

Laura set the pack down, straps up and ready to go. She moved to her knees and told Abby to get ready to run. If Seth came to them already running, they would be ready to join him.

Laura kept her eyes on the area Seth had disappeared into when he left her and Abby. She assumed he would come back from the same direction. She hoped he would approach them slowly and steadily, the same way he had left. She hoped he would return and tell her everything was going to be okay. That the distraction would happen soon. She hoped he would pick up Abby, and she could shoulder the pack. Laura hoped they could hold hands and wait. And then run. Together. As one. As planned.

Hopes were nice. They had seen Laura through many dark times. But these hopes all died as the earth literally moved. Something big had just blown up. The men all jumped up. There was yelling. Questions. Smoke rose from the part of the forest where Seth had disappeared with the contents of that box. The men ran toward it then. All of them. The camp was empty and there was a clear path to those rafts.

But where was Seth? Was he hurt? Was he unable to make a delayed explosion and so he sacrificed himself for them?

Was she supposed to run to those rafts without him? *No, Lord. Please.* If she ran now and he was hurt or coming, then he would be left behind. If she did not run now and those men came back, then she and Abby would be caught. Those men had to know they were in the area. That explosion was clearly not an accident.

What am I supposed to do, God? Help me. I don't know what to do!

Laura was looking between the rafts and the place where Seth should be coming from.

She stood up. Picked up Abby. Indecision ripped her soul into pieces.

It wasn't supposed to be like this.

And then she finally saw Seth. He was running, full steam, toward her. "Go! Go! Run, Laura!"

And she did. She started running, ignoring the shakiness in her legs from those moments where she thought Seth wasn't coming. Seth caught up to her and took Abby out of her arms without breaking stride.

They reached the rafts. Seth set Abby down and grabbed one. Placed it on the river bank and then put Abby inside. They were getting ready to push it in the water. To push and jump and hold on, when Laura heard the first gunshot.

Aimed at them.

She turned and saw several large, angry men running their way. And they were shooting as they came.

Seth didn't know if he was irritated his explosion didn't wait until he was back to Laura before going off or proud that he had managed to make it go boom at all. That crate had not been full of the ordinances of Seth's dreams. He'd had to take apart several smaller weapons and use their parts to make an explosive device. He'd also had to rig up some kind of fuse to get any delay at all.

He'd done his best, but he'd known, he had just known, that it would not be good enough. That was okay. When he was running back to Laura, when he heard the explosion happen much earlier than it should have, he had known that she would probably leave without him. And, with that knife, she would probably take away the option of him using another raft to follow.

And that was okay. He was running, using his legs for all they were worth, feeling the pain from the old injury jolt in his knees as he pushed even harder, and he was okay. Laura and Abby would make it to safety. They would go down that river and away from these guys and past the fire. They could ride until they reached help. And Seth would know that he had done a good and honorable job.

Dying was not a new concept. Dying in an unexpected and painful way wasn't new, either. Seth had come to terms with the choices he made in his life.

He had lost that peace for a while, back home. How ironic that it was the safety of home and the love of his family that had taken away his blasé acceptance of what was to come. And he had run. But he had fixed that as much as possible. Laura would help him make amends and his family would have some kind of closure.

So Seth had run and run and run. Even though it was pointless. Even though he was too late and he had missed his chance. But Laura would have hers. He ran, rounding that corner, fully prepared to see two destroyed rafts and one missing raft. And he was ready to thank God for that, to thank Him that Laura and her sweet girl would make it. To give thanks and then to fight until he couldn't fight anymore.

He'd almost fallen over when he took that corner and saw Laura and Abby. Standing there. They were just standing there looking at him. Why were they just standing there when the explosion had gone off minutes ago? He'd yelled, as loud as he could. There was no point in trying to be covert. Not if Laura and Abby never made it to the rafts.

They'd pushed the raft into the water, skipping the step where they disabled the other rafts. There just wasn't time.

Then the bullets came. One hit a rock that sat halfway in the water. The rock burst into little pieces, tiny shards of warning that their time was well and truly up. They needed to get in that raft and get speeding down the river or they would not be going anywhere.

Those men would catch Laura and Abby and they would kill them. That could not happen.

No.

Abby was on her stomach in the raft, her little body as close to the floor as it could be. She was holding on to some of the inner ties. Good girl. Laura must have told her what to do and she was doing it perfectly. Such a smart and good girl.

It took three shoves to get the raft in the water, and the shots behind them didn't stop. Seth did not know how none of them hit the raft or him and Laura. No, that wasn't true. He did know. He always knew who protected him in this world.

Laura and Seth jumped in the raft before the current could carry it away and Seth was thankful yet again for Laura's outdoor skills. She knew exactly what to do and Seth did not have to worry about her in that respect. They each picked up the oars that were lying next to Abby and began to paddle. The current was powerful, so if they could get the raft floating they would be okay.

They should be okay.

They would have a fighting chance at least.

And a fighting chance was all they needed to make it.

"Stay as low as possible." He had to yell to be heard over the noise of the water all around them. He could see the men running toward them, guns still pulled. The closer they got, the better their chances of actually hitting their target.

"I didn't think you were coming." Seth jerked his gaze away from the men and looked at Laura. Her voice was pure anguish. Absolute pain. She was…she was…crying.

Seth gripped the oar harder and used every bit of strength the adrenaline rush had given him to paddle, willing the raft to move faster. They needed to be away from these men. They needed to be down this river. To be safe, so Seth could hug Laura and reassure her and do whatever he needed to do to make that look leave her face. To make that tone go away. It was unacceptable that she was feeling this way. Unacceptable, and Seth needed to fix it.

They both jerked down at the sound of a

gunshot that was much, much closer than the others had been. Too close.

He looked and saw a Jeep speeding along, tracking them on land while their raft tried to run away downriver. The Jeep was going very fast and the ground was bumpy, so the man standing up in the back and trying to kill them wasn't able to aim accurately.

Another shot. Seth flinched again.

He might not be able to get a clear shot off, but he was sure getting close enough. Seth pulled his own gun and returned fire. His shot didn't land, but the Jeep did swerve a bit, so that was good. Something. Better than nothing.

Seth turned and saw Laura struggling with the oar. He immediately put his gun back in its holster and resumed working with his oar. The current provided momentum. They were going plenty fast, and though Seth wanted to get away he didn't really want to go any faster. This raft already felt like an out-of-control amusement park ride.

No, they weren't using the oars for speed. They were using them to navigate around the obstacles in the water. Rocks, tree branches, rocks, rocks and rocks. They were high up in the Rocky Mountains and this part of the country was aptly named.

Abby was wet, very wet. Seth could see her shivering. All the water that sloshed into the raft as they pushed against rocks with their oars and encountered the churning liquid landed on the floor of the raft. Where Abby was. But she was still holding on. Laura was sitting with one leg over the child, helping to hold her in place.

Seth worried about Abby drowning, but she was on her side. Her face was clear of the water on the floor. And down there was safer than the alternative.

He flinched as another shot came from the Jeep. And then another.

This needed to stop. One of those shots was going to land. Seth knew it. Statistics said it would land eventually and the shooter was not giving up. Seth looked down the river, almost hoping to see the active fire. They needed to get to that part, where the Jeep could no longer follow.

Seth saw smoke, but no flames. The river was windy at this part, so it could be around the next bend. It could be close. *Please, God, let it be close.*

"Seth!" Laura's scream was just as an-

guished as her last statement. He looked to
where she was pointing. At a raft. Following
them down the river. It had four men in it
and they were close enough that Seth could
see the murderous expressions on their faces.

And the guns in their hands.

THIRTEEN

When Laura had first seen those rafts, she'd thought they were God's way of answering her prayers. Now she thought they were the physical embodiment of every nightmare she had ever had. They should have tried to sneak around the barricade. Or to go through the fire. Either of those options suddenly seemed better and more reasonable to Laura than their current predicament.

It couldn't be possible, but it seemed like the men on the raft behind them were catching up. Even though they were in the same water, with the same type of boat, theirs looked like it was going faster.

Laura closed her eyes, squeezing the handle of her oar until the pain cut through the numbness. They had four large men in that raft. Each man had an oar. Those men were not using their oars to avoid rocks. They were using them to propel the raft through the water.

The raft was going to capture them.

It was going to catch up and then they would shoot Seth. They looked angry enough that they might shoot Laura and Abby, too, no matter what Mahoney had said.

This was going to end badly.

But she wasn't about to give up. "Seth, they are all using their oars to go faster. The raft is going to catch up with us."

Seth didn't respond to her yell, but the look on his face showed that he either heard her or he had realized the same thing.

The Jeep was still following on the side of the river. The man in the back was yelling into some kind of radio. He was talking instead of shooting. That couldn't be good.

What was he planning? Why had he stopped shooting?

"Laura! Look! The fire!"

Laura looked and saw. The fire. They had rounded several curves in the macabre pinball game they were playing, and the flames from the fire were now very visible. Laura thought she could feel the heat, but that was probably her imagination.

The flames moved and danced and Laura

had to force herself to look at the river, to focus on the boulders there. Those large, hard obstacles were every bit as much a threat as the men with guns who followed them on land and water.

The only good thing about getting ready to raft through a fire was that the Jeep would have to stop. That would take away an attack from at least one side.

"Laura. Get down. Now." Seth's voice was somehow low and deadly and still loud enough to carry to her. She looked ahead and saw a second Jeep parked on the side of the river, at the spot right before the flames were consuming the mountain.

It was parked and waiting.

There were several men standing by it.

With guns.

Pointed at them.

That was what the Jeep man had been doing. Radioing for backup. Backup that wasn't hindered by being in a moving Jeep traveling over uneven ground. Backup that could probably hit its target.

And they were the target.

Laura got down as much as possible. She moved so that both of her legs were over Abby, and she could feel her child's heat under her thighs. Getting down to avoid getting shot meant the raft was going to hit more rocks.

Seth handed her his oar. "Hold this. I'll shoot better with two hands, but I don't want to lose my oar."

Laura clung to the handle, pairing it up with hers. She had them both pulled inside the raft, clutching them like some kind of shield. Too bad they weren't bulletproof. She crouched down as low as possible, shoving the oars under one armpit and holding them with one hand. Laura reached down with the other hand and held on to Abby. She tried to make her hand gentle and reassuring, but she doubted her girl felt anything but terrified.

This was not the kind of childhood a little girl should have. How had it come to this? All Laura had wanted to do was get off this mountain and live a normal life. Be a normal girl. Normal.

Yet, here she was. Back on this mountain. Widowed. Running for her life. Dragging her child through one traumatic experience after another. It wasn't supposed to be like this. It wasn't supposed to be like this at all.

She looked up from her crouch and saw Seth holding one of the raft ties in his fist.

She knew he was hoping to secure himself to the raft, but the sight didn't make her feel better at all. He couldn't wrap it around his wrist or hand because if he went over that could really hurt him. But she didn't think he would be able to hold on, either. It was just too much to ask of a human being. Right now, the sight of him holding that rope felt very useless to Laura. Pointless. And depressing.

She flinched at the sound of the first shot. Suppressed a scream. Heard Abby cry out.

Then there was a second shot. A third. Coming from Seth. From that parked Jeep. From the raft behind them. Back and forth, and all too loud and too close.

The raft was jerking, bouncing off of boulders. Slamming into waves. Those movements were painful and terrifying and probably the only reason that the men on the riverbank or raft behind them had not managed to shoot them yet.

Seth fired one more time and then he stopped. He slid over to where Laura was and shielded her body with his. He was around her and over her and covering her and Abby much more than Laura would have thought was possible. "I hit the other raft, but I didn't do anything to the men on the shore.

I'm out of bullets. We're almost to the fire line. Almost."

Almost. Almost. Almost. Laura chanted the words in her head. They were a plea. And a prayer. They had come so far, they had to make it through this, too. They just had to.

The weight of Seth's body increased and Laura was almost lying down on top of Abby. The water in the bottom of the raft was freezing and they were all soaking wet. None of that stopped Laura from feeling the heat, though. It came out of nowhere, though really it had been their end goal all along. They were past the fire line.

The bullets stopped. That horrible popping noise that made Laura tense every muscle waiting to see if a bullet would hit its mark. It was gone.

But it wasn't quiet. The fire was every bit as alive and growling as the water. The men in the Jeep had been intent on killing them. This fire seemed intent on killing anything. Everything. In its path or not. It was hungry, and they were nothing more than fuel.

About a minute after the last shot was fired, Seth sat up. He grabbed one of the oars that Laura was holding and moved back to the front of the raft. Now that they were done fighting the men, they only had to fight the river. And a fire.

The river was substantial, but the flames were jumping toward it. They needed to stay away from that side. Laura positioned her own oar and started helping. It was a relief to be proactive when it came to all these boulders. The repetitive jarring of slamming into rock after rock lessened.

Laura's arms began to ache with the effort she was expending, but it felt good. She was alive, and she was still fighting. Her eyes began to water, maybe from the heat. Maybe from the wind.

She gazed at the part of the mountain on the other side of the river. It looked dry. And, most important, not on fire. It was so tempting to try to navigate over there. To try to stop, get out, walk on her legs. Make Abby dry and warm.

But that was not an option. It wasn't safe to try to land the raft over there. Those men were not giving up. How long would it take them to cross the river and come down the mountain? Though it was bumpy and cold and flat-out miserable, this river was still the fastest route down. It was still their best shot at getting off this mountain and to help.

Laura could only see Seth's back. And more fire. Up ahead, for as far as she could see, fire. Flames and heat and fire and the consumption of this mountain she loved so much.

Her dad's part of the mountain. His refuge.

Her part of the mountain. Her refuge.

The river curved and Laura actually sobbed when she saw that the fire had burned out up ahead. She hadn't even realized she was crying until those tears became a fountain of emotion. Seth turned to look at her, and she just pointed. His smile was somber, but it was there. He turned back around to face the front again and Laura reached down to pat Abby on the back.

She smiled at the girl. "It's going to be okay, Abby. We're almost done with the worst part."

As quickly as it appeared, that heat ended. Smoke was still heavy in the air, but Laura glanced over to where the sky looked blue. She imagined the town at the base. The town that this river was taking them to. The town full of people, and not the kind who wanted to kill them. The kind who could help to keep Abby safe.

This was going to be okay.

"Laura!" Seth's tone told her that she was wrong. This was not going to be okay. He leaned to the side, and she looked up ahead. There were several large trees lying across the river. There was no way to get around. Their raft would hit nature's equivalent of a brick wall.

This wasn't happening.

Okay, it was. And, frankly, Seth didn't know why he was surprised. This week was going down in history as one of the worst weeks ever. And he said that as a man who had fought in a brutal war, been injured and run away from his family. Yeah. This week had been that bad.

"Go right. Try to go right." He had to turn around to make sure Laura heard him. She immediately started trying to push the raft that way. He did, too. But it wasn't enough. Even with their combined efforts, their skilled efforts, the raft was resisting any attempt to go toward the side of the river that had not been burned by the fire.

"Seth, it's too hard. The current is working against us." She was right of course. He should have realized sooner. Much of their ride down so far had involved trying to stay away from the side of the mountain that was on fire. Because the raft wanted to list that way.

"The left. Go to the left." His aching muscles almost appreciated the change in exertion.

And it was working. It was absolutely working. The raft moved over to the bank, hitting some of the smaller rocks lining that side. They were in the right position now. They just needed to slow down.

Just.

"Seth, look. We can use that to ramp up on the bank." Laura was pointing to a place up ahead where the bank dipped in. Made a little inlet. Yes, this could work.

Seth tensed his arms as they approached the inlet. He used every bit of strength he could muster and pushed toward it. He heard Laura give a yell as she pushed, too.

And the raft was stopped. They were in the inlet. Seth quickly scrambled out, taking one of the raft ties with him. He pulled it taut and looked over to tell Laura to follow.

But she was already there with Abby. She pushed the child ahead of her, half carrying her as she climbed over the end edge of the raft onto dry land.

Once they were off, Seth started to pull the raft out of the water. He looked up in surprise when Laura stepped in front of him, grabbed the rope and began pulling, too. The raft came out of the water. Once it was fully on the ground, with no chance of it being sucked back in, Seth let go.

He sank down to his knees on the ground and watched Laura do the same. She held her arms out to Abby, and the little girl ran to her mom. Abby threw herself at Laura with such force that both mother and child ended up lying on the ground.

Seth crawled over to where Laura was and flopped on his back next to her. She was holding Abby on top of her body, the little girl looking almost like a blanket. A shaking blanket. Seth couldn't hear the crying, but Abby was clearly sobbing into her mother's neck.

And neither one of them said a word.

They just stayed there, breathing heavily, shivering, trying to soak up every sunray that was available.

After what felt like one minute and one hour all at once, Seth rolled over and looked at Laura. She turned her head toward him.

"Well, that was fun," she said. "Let's do that again the week after never."

Seth smiled at her humor. All of this, and she was still here with him. "So, you're saying that you don't want to carry this raft to the other side of the wall of trees and get back in?" His tone was light, but his question was very much a serious one. They were not out of the woods yet. Neither literally nor metaphorically.

She looked at Abby, who was still on top of her. Laura's hands were back to rubbing again, more soothing motions that were probably also meant to help the child warm up.

"What do you think, Seth? I really don't want to get back in the raft. It's dangerous and cold. Abby is so tired, I'm afraid that she'll get hurt."

She wasn't wrong. Again. "We were really fortunate with that first ride. Really favored. I agree—let's walk."

Laura sat up, keeping Abby in her lap, the child still plastered to her chest. "Okay. Let's go. The sooner we start, the sooner we'll reach town."

Seth wanted to build a fire and warm them up. He wanted to get them out of those wet clothes. He wanted to let them rest. And he really wanted to take off his boots and take the world's longest nap. But he could do none of those things. He could only stand up, hold out a hand to help pull Laura to her feet and then reach out and take Abby.

He didn't ask this time. He just took the little girl, and she came without protest from either mom or child. She was trembling slightly in Seth's arms and he held her closer to his body, hoping his heat would both warm and calm her.

"I don't even want to think about how we spent the better part of two days walking up this mountain and we just undid all that work in minutes." Her voice sounded tired. Really tired.

"I know. But we're okay. And we're clear of those men." He wanted to reassure her. "Plus, we're walking downhill now. This is good."

"We're past the point where the cabin was. It's probably gone, huh?"

Seth really wished that he was okay with lying to her. But he wouldn't do that. Not to anyone, but especially not to her. "I don't know, Laura. But you're probably right. It's probably damaged at best."

She was silent, and Seth tried to give her time to process, focusing on leading them downhill on the easiest path he could find. Abby had stopped shivering. Her head was heavy on his shoulder, and Seth looked down to see her eyes were closed. She was sleeping.

Something moved in his chest as he pondered the gift that was carrying a sleeping child. A little girl who trusted him enough to let go of any worry or fear. Who trusted that he would make everything okay and all she had to do was close her eyes and go to sleep.

I'm not going to let her down, Lord. I'm not going to let either one of them down. Help me. Let us feel your presence. Keep these three people safe.

"Seth?" Laura's voice was soft, and he thought he heard tears in it. He tightened his arms around Abby to stop himself from reaching out to Laura.

"Yeah?"

"I'm really glad you're here. I thought I wanted to be all alone with Abby, but I was wrong. I was really wrong. A person isn't meant to go through life isolated from others."

Seth stopped walking and closed his eyes. This woman reached right inside him and just pierced his heart. The one he had tried so hard to turn to stone. It wasn't stone. It was soft. And bleeding.

He opened his eyes and looked at her. "I'm glad I'm here, too, Laura." It was the truth. And it was the very surface of all the things he felt swirling around inside his heart and mind. He just needed some time, preferably off this mountain and somewhere safe, to consider them. Understand what they meant.

They walked, then. And walked some more. It was the continuing theme of this journey so far. Seth figured they had to be getting close to something. To the bottom or to people or to something. Laura's mountain was remote and covered a large area but it did not go down indefinitely. They had to be off it. He turned to ask Laura if she recognized where they were when Abby moved.

"Mama!" Abby lifted her head and reached out for her mom. Seth felt an intense sense of loss as Laura took the girl and she was no longer cradled against his chest.

"Hey there, pretty girl, did you have a nice nap?" Laura was murmuring into Abby's ear, but Seth could hear every word. And he could sense the maternal love that Laura radiated when she was with her child.

Seth felt the burn before he heard the shot.

The impact of the bullet knocked him off his feet. He heard Laura and Abby scream, but all he could see was the sky. It was blue again. The smoke was blowing up the mountain, and from right here it looked like a beautiful day.

Laura was kneeling over him, pushing down on his chest so hard that he groaned. Why was she hurting him? He moved his hands to where Laura's were and felt something warm and wet. Blood. His blood.

"Laura. Run. You and Abby need to run."

Her expression could only be described as horrified. "No. No, Seth."

He grabbed her wrists. Pulled them away. "Go. The shooter will be coming. You have to save Abby."

His vision was blurring, but he saw the tears rolling down her cheek. She looked at him with anguish in her eyes, regret tightening her mouth. She nodded. "Thank you. I'm so sorry."

The she bent down and kissed him. It was the best thing he had ever felt. He wanted it to last forever.

No. She needed to run.

She lifted her lips and put her hand over her mouth. Seth turned his head and watched her pick up Abby and start to run.

The dark spots in his vision were dancing. Growing bigger. But he kept his eyes on Laura and Abby, willing them to run and run and run until they simply disappeared.

Laura made it twenty feet when a group of men stepped out of the trees right in front of her. She froze.

"Hello, Ms. Donovan. You've made this all much harder than it needed to be. Tried to ruin my plans. But you'll be glad to know that I think I can salvage them." The man standing in the middle spoke with a condescending tone. He wasn't armed, but he didn't need to be. The other men with him were armed enough for everyone.

Seth tried to yell, to distract them. To plead with them. To do…something. His words were a harsh whisper. They did nothing.

Seth watched the man walk up and put his hand on Laura's cheek. Reach over and stroke Abby's hair, even though Laura tried to jerk her daughter away from that touch.

Seth had messed up, and it was too late to fix it.

They should have risked riding the raft the rest of the way down.

Then black spots became all that there was.

FOURTEEN

Laura needed to stay calm to get out of this situation. Calm. She needed to be calm.

That was impossible. Seth was bleeding into the forest somewhere. Or not. Maybe he had stopped bleeding. Maybe he was dead. Laura bit the side of her tongue until the pain added to her tears. She wasn't going to think like that. Seth was okay. Seth had to be okay.

Except, she knew he wasn't. Mahoney had walked over to him, and Laura feared he was going to let the man who called dibs finish it. To kill Seth. Instead, he had laughed and said to leave Seth. To let him die a slow death.

No. Please, please, please. Please, God. Let Seth be okay.

Abby made a little squeak and Laura realized she was holding her too tight. She lessened the pressure of her arms. "Sorry, baby. Mama's sorry."

For so much. Much, much more than a tight hug.

They were sitting on what used to be a chair in her home. The boss's men had used their guns to get Laura and Abby into yet another Jeep. A gun pointed at her daughter made Laura startlingly eager to do whatever was asked of her. Whatever she was told—ordered to do.

Laura couldn't identify the emotions at seeing her cabin again. The forest all around was destroyed. But this cabin. It was safe. It was whole. Well, for the most part, anyway. The fire had come in. Touched some things. Left. But most of her belongings were salvageable.

Mahoney had laughed at her expression. "Yeah. I saved it. Couldn't have it going up in flames empty, could I? Good thing my guys were prepared."

He'd pointed to the chair and Laura had sat. Ten minutes later, she still felt…nothing. Numb. Too numb even for the terror to come through.

But it was there. She had Abby on her lap. Had both arms wrapped tight around her. Was clutching her and vowing to protect her daughter with everything she had.

Right now, Abby felt an awful lot like a

shield. Like whatever tried to hurt Laura would have to go through Abby.

Laura hated that. Numb or not, she could feel her skin crawling with the realization that her daughter was protecting her in a very real way. She wanted to move Abby from her lap. From in front of her chest. But where would she put her? Wasn't she safer in her mother's arms than anywhere else? That should be the safest place in the world for a little girl.

But if this man chose to shoot her, to shoot her in the same place where he shot Seth, that bullet would have to go through Abby to get to her.

Suddenly, Laura wasn't numb. She was feeling everything all at once. Hot and cold and terror. The urge to run. To flee. To hide. The need to fall to her knees, both to beg God and to beg this man.

Please, please, please. Don't hurt my baby. Not my baby.

Laura wanted to offer herself. To see if she could be enough of a sacrifice to appease this man. But, if she was, if he chose only to hurt her and not Abby, then where would her daughter be? How could she survive left alone on this mountain?

They had spent days, literally, trying to get

away from Mahoney. Running and hiding. Praying. Planning. Using every bit of physical and mental energy that they had.

It didn't matter. None of it mattered. Laura and Abby were right back where they started. And, Seth. Seth was, well, not here. Maybe not alive.

No. No, no, no.

This was not happening.

Laura stood up, still clutching Abby. All the men in the room turned toward her. All with guns drawn. Laura swallowed, but she just knew she would go insane if she had to sit and wait and wonder. She couldn't take the possibilities anymore.

"Sit back down, Mrs. Donovan. Right now." Mahoney did not sound upset, but he still sounded deadly. His hand held the gun like he knew what he was doing with it. That hand wasn't shaking. It looked awfully sure and ready.

"Why? You're just going to kill us anyway, aren't you? Like you did Seth?"

"I am. But I would really prefer it looked like an accident."

Anger rushed a course of fire across Laura's face. "Yeah. And I'd really prefer that someone knows we were killed. That someone looks for our killer. That someone comes after you."

Laura swallowed a sob. She could do this. She had to. It had come down to this, and it was time for her to leave Abby in Jesus's hands and trust that He would protect her. Laura swallowed again, determined to not talk to this man with a trembling or weak voice. He probably knew that he had gotten to her, but she refused to give him the evidence of that fact.

"Besides, you already shot Seth. The authorities are going to know there was a murderer up on the mountain."

Mahoney lowered his gun and smiled at the man standing to his left. Laura noticed that none of the other men had lowered their weapons even a fraction.

"Oh, I disagree, Mrs. Donovan. Killing the ranger wasn't ideal, but you're the one who brought him into this. And when the authorities look into his death, they will have no reason to ever connect him to me. Especially since you and your daughter will have died in this unfortunate fire."

Laura felt herself glaring, but this wasn't an ideal time to physically attack the man. For one, she'd have to put Abby down. For two, well, she didn't have a two. All she cared about, all she knew, was that she had to figure out a way to save Abby.

That wasn't true. She still cared about Seth. So much. He was also struggling with his own regrets. He'd had been with her these last few days. She did not want him to die.

And for a woman who had wanted to sit in the dark and hide after her husband died, Laura found that she cared very much about her own future, too. But she could not help Seth. She couldn't even help herself. Maybe, just maybe, she could help Abby.

Please, God. Please let this work.

"I want my daughter to survive this. She's young. Too young. She'll never remember what happened. Or what you looked like. Your name. If you drop her off in town, make sure she is found, she can still live a full life. And she won't be any kind of threat to you."

Laura swallowed several times in a row. Her daughter. Her baby. She hopefully wouldn't remember the terror of this week. But she wouldn't remember Laura, either. She wouldn't remember that she was wanted and loved. That her mother did not leave her willingly.

"Ah, Mrs. Donovan, you're touching my heart. Really, I'm feeling it right here." He tapped his chest, where his heart would be. Laura didn't think he had one, though. He couldn't. "And what would convince me to take your child to safety after I kill you?"

Laura forced herself to ignore the part where he confirmed that he was actually going to kill her. She already knew that, but it still didn't feel good to hear him say it out loud. "Because you're not an evil man." He was. He really was. But she was desperate.

Mahoney crossed his arms over his chest and looked at Laura. His eyes were narrowed and his mouth was a rigidly straight line. "I do not like being manipulated, Mrs. Donovan. I like to be in charge. I am always in charge."

Laura met his gaze. She wasn't going to look away from this man. And, if she was going to die, she wanted to know why. "How did you know Josh? What did you do to him?"

Mahoney smiled. "Oh, your Joshua was one of my best employees."

Laura sat down. She was breathing as slowly as possible, trying to stop the tears.

Mahoney sat across from her. He leaned back in his chair, crossing the ankle of one suit-clad leg over the knee of the other. He looked comfortable, as though they were discussing the weather instead of her husband's attachment to a criminal. "I'll be brief, Mrs. Donovan. I've had an eventful few days, and I'm actually quite ready to get back to the comforts of my home. I'm a drug dealer. A really, really good one."

Laura stared at him with her eyes so wide that her skin felt stretched.

"I'm also a man of business. And I like things to be—" he quirked his lips at Laura and she swallowed back even more bile "—neat. I needed help with my money, and so I hired the best."

No. Laura knew where he was going now. He had hired Josh?

"Ah, you're catching on. My private detectives told me that you were smart. I can see they were correct. Yes, I hired your husband's firm. He handled my account. He was excellent at what he did."

"Josh wasn't a criminal. He wasn't." It seemed ridiculous to argue this point, but Laura couldn't help herself. This man would never convince her that Josh had been involved with the drug trade.

"No. Sadly for all of you, he was not. He worked for me for several years, and all was well. Then, somehow, he realized something was, shall we say, amiss. I did not know it at the time, but he started gathering evidence of my misdeeds. He was going to turn me in to the authorities."

Yes. That was the Josh that Laura had known.

"Thankfully, I discovered what he was doing. I'm a careful man. I have certain, ah, safeguards in place. And they protected me."

Laura was back to glaring. He sounded so proud of his criminal system.

"Once I became aware, I took actions to eliminate the threat. I had an associate kill your husband."

There was a roaring in her ears. It sounded like a train. And a wail. He'd just told her he killed her husband. He said it like it was nothing. Like he washed his car and picked up pizza for dinner.

"Unfortunately, my associate was a bit hasty. He killed young Joshua before finding the papers."

"Papers?" Laura didn't know what he was talking about, but that might have been because her brain was stuck back on the part about how he killed her husband and destroyed her life.

"Keep up, Mrs. Donovan. I dislike having

to repeat myself. Your husband collected papers proving my guilt. It would be quite difficult for me if those papers landed in the wrong hands."

"Like the police."

"Exactly."

"The safe-deposit box," she whispered. That key she had found.

"We had looked everywhere. We even searched your home."

Laura's throat was almost too tight to talk. "My home?"

Mahoney looked almost rueful. "Oh, yes. While you were at young Joshua's funeral. We did not find the papers anywhere."

Laura was going to throw up. "I've been wanting to know. How did you know about the key?"

Mahoney's face tightened. "We've been watching you. Waiting. Thinking that eventually you would take the papers to the authorities. But you never did."

They had been watching her, even up on the mountain. Seth had been right. Of course he had been. The logical answer was usually the true answer. Was the feeling of safety ever real?

"We've been monitoring calls—both your

phone and Joshua's firm," Mahoney said. "You called them last week, asking about the key."

She really was the reason Mahoney was here.

"Once I knew you had the key to the box that held those papers," Mahoney continued, "I had to plan a way to get to you. It turned out that my preparation really paid off." More anger in his voice. "You and that park ranger made this much more difficult than it needed to be."

Laura's own anger bubbled and roiled.

"But I have you where I want you now. And this will all be over in a minute."

The bubbling and roiling froze and Laura's blood was ice.

For a second, Seth thought he was stuck in yet another dream about Afghanistan. The only thing he could feel was the acid inside his body, eating away at what was left of his soul. And he was alone, all alone.

Seth opened his eyes and sucked in a ragged breath. Smoke. Wetness. Rocky ground. He wasn't in his bed having another nightmare. He was up on Laura's mountain. And she and Abby weren't here.

The men. Seth jerked as the full implication hit him. Those men had Laura and Abby. They took them. Why did they take them if they were just going to kill them? Where were they now?

Slowly, Seth turned on his side. He took a couple of deep breaths and tried to assess what his body was telling him. Beyond the pain. Beyond the shock. After a minute, he sat up. He saw Laura's pack on the ground not too far away. It had either fallen or been thrown there. Seth tried not to picture that scene, what it had looked like when those men had taken them.

Seth crawled to the pack and opened it. Laura had lightened it up before making that run to the rafts. He rummaged around and smiled. The first-aid kit was still in there. That woman was an expert survivalist and she knew how to prioritize. Thank you, Laura Donovan.

Hs hand froze when he saw Abby's Duckie. That sweet girl was scared somewhere. She needed her Duckie. She needed Seth.

Seth groaned and slowly took off his shirt. The bleeding had slowed and the entry wound was crusty on the outside. How long had he been out? Seth tried to reach his hand around to his back, but that wasn't happening. He could feel blood running down his back, so the bullet had exited. At least it wasn't still inside.

Seth shouldn't be alive. Those men were pros. Why wasn't he dead?

Seth looked down and felt his breath catch. His dog tags. He'd had them on under his shirt. They'd been a part of him for so long, had seen him through so much. He still wore them every day, even though he had left military service far behind.

They were a mess. Not just covered in blood, but...dented? Seth quickly took them off, examining them with his eyes and fingers. They'd been hit. With a bullet.

It was impossible that they saved his life. But here he was, alive. The bullet should have killed him. They must have slowed it down. Maybe changed its path. He didn't know. All that mattered is that he was still alive.

Seth bandaged his wounds as best he could and then crawled to where he saw a large stick. Using it as a makeshift cane, he slowly stood up. This was doable. Seth knew what it felt like to be dying, and this wasn't it.

He wouldn't say he was in good shape, but he was much better than he should be, all things considered. Leaning on the stick, Seth looked around. He did not see or hear anything except the normal forest sights and sounds.

Mahoney must have taken them back to the cabin. To kill them there. That was the only thing that made any kind of sense.

Seth looked up the mountain. That's where Laura's cabin was. That's where the fire was. That's where Mahoney had wanted to kill her and Abby to begin with. He swallowed and took a couple steps in that direction. That was probably where Laura was. The helicopter could have left while Seth was unconscious. But if it hadn't, then Laura and Abby were up there.

Seth took a few more steps and had to stop again. Going uphill was not easy at the best of times, but especially not with a hole going through his body. He'd have to go through the fire again. And when he got there, then what? It would be him against a large number of armed men. Men who were not injured.

Seth wanted to go up. He wanted to charge up that mountain and save Laura and Abby. Save the day. He wanted to know that they were safe because he made them safe. That the bad guys were captured because he captured them.

Seth wanted to climb the mountain and be the hero. Do it all himself.

He sat down on a large rock, dropped the stick and leaned forward, resting his elbows on his thighs and holding his head. It hurt, bent over like this, but it hurt even more when Seth realized what he was thinking.

Do it all by himself. Isn't that how he got here in the first place? Isn't that what he counted as one of his greatest regrets? He didn't want his family to help him recover. He didn't want to admit weakness. No, he left so he could do it all by himself.

And it had been a mistake. He should have stayed. He should have leaned on those who loved him. He should have let them help.

No. He wasn't making that mistake again. He needed to go down the mountain. Away from Laura and Abby.

It felt an awful lot like he was running away and leaving them to take care of themselves.

But it was the right move. The hard move, but the right one. It gave Laura and Abby the greatest chance of surviving whatever it was they were enduring right now.

Seth stood and started walking down the mountain. He turned each step into a prayer.

Let me find help.

Let Laura and Abby be okay.

Don't let them be afraid.

Comfort them.

Help them feel loved.

Don't let me be too late.

Please, God.

Please.

The prayers were a rhythm, his heart bleeding into his pleas to God. He didn't feel the pain of his injuries. He didn't consider how far away help might be. He didn't look at the setting sun or the dark shadows that surrounded him. He only looked at the ground about three feet in front of him. Made sure he placed each foot securely. Firmly on the ground. Held on to his cane and begged God to find Laura and Abby in this mess and be with them.

His mom would have chastised him for that prayer. She believed that God was always with you. No one needed to ask God to be with a hurting person, because He never left. Ever. Instead, she would have told Seth to pray for the hurting person to be aware of God's presence. To open themselves up enough to feel it and to take comfort in it.

Seth almost missed a step as a longing for his mom caught him off guard. He should have called her. He'd written that his leaving was his fault. Not hers. His demons to face. Not her mistakes. Not her anything. But he should have called his mother.

Seth coughed and intentionally cleared his head. No. Laura and Abby didn't need his regrets over his past mistakes. They needed his prayers. And his help. Both came with him taking this next step. Then the one after that. And the next one.

Seth walked for forever. He started to wonder if he was maybe still on the forest floor unconscious. Maybe this was a nightmare where he walked and walked and walked but never reached his destination.

Maybe he should have gone up the mountain. To the fire at least. There might have been emergency personnel there, fighting the blaze. They could have helped.

The fire was closer than the bottom of this never-ending slope.

He should have gone up.

Seth stopped walking and looked back up the mountain. The scent of smoke had faded.

He could not see any. Had they finally managed to put the blaze out? Or was he that far away?

Should he continue on? Maybe he should reverse course. Maybe going down was yet another mistake, but he still had time to fix it.

Seth was frozen. He didn't know which way to walk, but he needed to move somewhere. Do something. Soon.

Seth was all alone in the forest.

FIFTEEN

Laura needed a plan. And a weapon. Her dad. Seth. Pretty much anything. And everything.

"Well, Mrs. Donovan, I won't say it's been fun. But I'll certainly remember you and all your spunk."

That compliment made Laura's skin crawl. He was going to get up, leave, and then they were going to die. The situation was unbearable. Laura was more afraid of watching her daughter be hurt than she was of dying. That's just how bad life had become. Death was the preferable outcome.

No. That was not true. She was her father's daughter. She was her Holy Father's daughter. She was a mom. Laura was smart and capable and more than willing to fight for her child's future. She needed to come up with a plan.

Which was exactly where this crazy internal monologue started.

Stall. She needed to figure out how to stay alive as long as possible. If there was any way at all that Seth was alive, he would come for them. Laura knew in the depths of her being that Seth would bring help. If he was alive.

If he wasn't alive. Well, then she needed to just try to stay living, and keep Abby alive and unhurt, for as long as possible. Maybe something would happen in the future to give them a fighting chance. So they needed a future.

The plan was to stall.

Now that she had a plan, Laura needed to figure out to how to execute it. And quickly, because Mahoney was getting ready to leave.

"Mr. Mahoney." It was the first time she had addressed him as anything formally. For a few extra minutes of life, she would be respectful toward this man. With her words at least, if not in her heart. "You're making a mistake. I can help you."

Mahoney moved to get up out of his chair, so Laura began to talk faster. "You're going to need me to get inside that safe-deposit box."

Mahoney smiled, fully standing. It was not a nice smile. "I have a copy of your husband's

death certificate. I have a copy of your iden-
tification. And I have a woman who looks
like she could be your twin. I don't need you
at all."

"You're wrong," she said.

Mahoney settled back down into his chair,
and some of the tension left Laura's muscles. Sitting was good. Sitting meant listening which meant taking up more time which
meant stalling. The plan was to hold things
up, and Laura intended to work that plan
until something better popped into her brain.
*Please, God, give me something better. Help
me to think my way out of this situation.*

Mahoney's eyes were narrowed and he
looked like he doubted her words. Well, she
doubted them, too. But it was all she had.

"What makes you say that?"

"I found a letter from my husband warning
me that the box was very important. I called
the bank and told them to make sure not to
let anyone but me inside. There's no way your
woman looks enough like me to pass careful scrutiny." That was a lie. All of it. Laura
hoped she was convincing.

"We've been monitoring your phone, Mrs.
Donovan. You did not call the bank. In fact,

you told Joshua's former secretary that you didn't know what bank the key was from."

Laura told herself to stay calm. Steady. And hopefully very convincing. "I found an envelope with a bank name on it the next day. I went back to town to make a call. My cell phone was dead, so I used Mr. Miller's phone at the general store."

Laura had gone back into town the very next day because her generator had died. She'd purchased the necessary part to fix it at the general store. But she had not made any phone calls.

Mahoney opened his briefcase and pulled out a large cell phone with a long antenna, probably a satellite phone. He made a call. "Yeah. Give me the rundown on what Laura Donovan did the day after she called the firm about that safe-deposit key."

Laura saw spots in her vision and forced herself to take a breath. She was thankful she had kept her lie close to the truth. The report Mahoney was hearing should match what she said. Should.

"Got it." Mahoney did not sound happy. He pushed a button on the phone, presumably disconnecting the call. Then he looked at her and his eyes were blazing. "Okay. Let's say you're telling the truth."

He bought it. "Take me with you. I'll get you the papers if you'll leave us alone after that." He wouldn't. Laura knew whatever he told her would be a lie. But it would buy them some time and that was good enough right now.

"And why didn't you mention any of this before?"

Laura's shame was not faked at all this time. "You told me that all you wanted was the key. You said if I gave it to you, that you would leave. That no one would get hurt. I believed you." Like a fool. She had given the man the thing he wanted without a second thought. He'd had a gun and he'd had her daughter and she had just caved. She was determined to be smarter this time.

Mahoney didn't say anything. He just stared at her for a long moment. Then he was back on his phone. "Yeah. I need to know about the phone calls made from that general store the second day that Laura Donovan went down there. From the owner's phone, too." Mahoney looked at Laura. "Last name Miller. Specifically, any banks that were called."

Laura forced her face to remain confident.

Why had she been so specific? And how quickly would Mahoney get the information and know she was lying?

Mahoney ended the call and leaned back in his chair. "We shouldn't have to wait too long. I don't think I believe you, but it never hurts to check. I've had men working since last week to track down the bank. That should be easier now that I have the key." Mahoney pulled out the gold key Laura had given him days ago. He waved it in front of her face before putting it back in his jacket's inside pocket. "I'm still thinking it will be best for all if you and your daughter die in a tragic accident and are quickly forgotten."

He planned to make it as though she and Abby were never here. Never lived. Tears rushed up behind Laura's eyes as she realized that she truly would disappear. No one would notice her absence. Or Abby's. Her family was all dead. Josh had been an only child of only children. His mom passed before Laura met him, and his dad passed their first year of marriage.

And Laura was really, really good at being alone. At not making friends. At pushing the few people who tried far, far away. Really, it was a wonder that Laura had ever met Josh. Known him. Loved him.

If she and her baby died, no one would visit their graves. Laura didn't even know if they would have graves.

This had been what she wanted. To be left alone. Loving people hurt, especially when they died and left. Her parents. Her dad. Josh. Everyone she loved had left her, and that was okay, because she wanted to be alone. Except she didn't. Laura didn't want that kind of life anymore, and she definitely did not want that for her sweet girl.

Laura wanted to attack this man. Her fists were aching with the pressure she was using to squeeze them into tight little balls. Abby was shaking, her head buried into Laura's shoulder, her arms squeezing Laura's neck tight. It almost felt like Abby was trying to climb inside Laura's body and hide there. Laura would let her if she could.

But Laura could not attack this man. She had to keep stalling and have faith. Faith in God. Faith in Seth. That was her mission right now.

Mahoney's cell phone rang, and he answered it. He was talking in a low voice, and he sounded pleased with whatever he was hearing.

Laura looked out the window, feeling desperation rising like a tsunami wave ready to wipe her out. She blinked hard at the shining reflection she saw.

A shining reflection. Like what had warned Seth about the men earlier. The warning that had allowed them to hide.

Laura knew her mountain, and she really knew her dad's cabin and the surrounding land. There wasn't anything out that window that would reflect light. And, since it was dark, there shouldn't be any light to reflect in the first place.

Maybe it was Mahoney's men. He had certainly brought enough men and equipment with him.

But maybe it wasn't.

Something was out in the woods. There was light. And it was reflecting. In a pattern. A very subtle pattern.

Laura looked away. At Mahoney. He was still on his phone, talking quickly and not paying any attention to her. Good.

Laura looked back out the window. That same reflection.

Could it be a clue? A signal? She didn't

know if that thought was blind hope or a reasonable conclusion. Either way, Laura was going to assume it meant something.

Mahoney put his phone back in his pocket and glared at her. "It seems you have a problem with your story, Mrs. Donovan."

It was a signal. Laura tightened her grip on Abby, and pictured all the ways out of this cabin. All the places she could hide. Something was going to happen. When it did, she would be ready.

"Problem?"

"Yes. There is—"

Her world exploded. Again. There were gunshots. Men yelling. Flashes of light and strange smells.

Laura jerked out of the chair, clutched Abby to her chest and ran. It was pure chaos, but Laura could navigate this cabin blind. If this was her chance, Abby's chance, she was going for it.

Seth was actually rocking back and forth on his feet to keep from running in. Joining the fight. The past two days had challenged him in ways that Afghanistan had never managed to do. But this? This standing here useless while others went in and fought to save

Laura and Abby—this waiting—might be the greatest challenge yet.

But waiting was best. He was here, but he was in no condition whatsoever to be fighting. The firefighters he'd encountered on his never-ending trip down this mountain had tried to make him go to the hospital. They'd called an ambulance and everything. Seth had thrown a fit he would not be proud of in the morning, refusing. Besides, he knew Laura's cabin better than any of them. He knew more about these men than they did. Bringing him along for his knowledge was the smart play.

Seth had stood by impatiently while the police arrived. While the necessary manpower was finally assembled. He had waited during that drive up to the outskirts of the cabin. He had waited while the SWAT team had done their reconnaissance. He had waited for them to come back and say whether Laura and Abby were even up here. If he was even in the right place. Then Seth had waited while the police had made their plan. And now? Now he was waiting while the good guys went in and fought the bad guys.

A fight where Laura and Abby would be caught in the middle. Caught in between flying bullets. Breaking glass. Smoke bombs.

Best-case scenario was they were hiding, terrified, waiting to see who won. Worst case involved that boss killing them to cut his losses. Or using them as hostages. Or them getting hit by a stray bullet. Or, or, or. It was too much.

Seth took a step forward. The jolt of pain made him stop. No. This was not about him. This was not about his pride or his ego. He would not be an asset right now. He would be a distraction. A liability. The best thing was for Seth to stand by.

Seth looked down at Duckie in his hands. The stuffed animal he wanted to put back in Abigail's arms.

Seth was absolutely sick of waiting.

And then, he wasn't waiting anymore. The shooting stopped. The area became as bright as day as the lights the police brought with them were turned on. Seth walked forward, taking in the scene.

There were a lot of men in cuffs sitting on the ground. The police were bringing more out of the house. More from behind the house.

And there was Mahoney. He had to be the boss. While all the other men were dressed in black gear, this man was wearing a suit. He did not have the look of a mercenary. No, he had the look of a sleazy businessman.

Seth took another step and made eye contact with the leader of the SWAT team. He nodded and Seth stopped hesitating. He rushed into the cabin as fast as his injured body would allow him.

Laura. Abby.

They weren't out front. Where were they?

He entered the cabin and ignored the destruction. He didn't care about broken furniture. No, he only cared about the two people who were hopefully safe inside.

"Laura! Abby! It's Seth. If you can hear me, come out now. It's safe." Seth took in another breath, preparing to yell again. If that didn't work, he would take this cabin apart and find every hidey-hole Malcolm Grant had put in it. He would find them.

"Abby! Wait!" Seth heard Laura's cry about a second before Abby came running into the room. She didn't slow down or pause before throwing herself against Seth's legs. Laura was right behind her.

Seth's legs gave out and he was on the floor. Abby crawled up his body, wrapping her arms around his neck and pressing her wet face against his cheek. He hugged her to his body, pushing Duckie into her hands. Laura leaned over and was suddenly pressed against him, too. Seth didn't know if she was trying to hug Abby or him, but it didn't matter. He opened his arms to include her, hugging both of them as hard as he could.

He sent one hand up to cup the back of Laura's head. He wanted to check them over to see if they were okay. He wanted to hold tight and never let go. He didn't even know what he wanted. This moment was all feeling.

"Seth, you're alive." Laura's voice was thick and Seth leaned his head back enough to see her face. She was crying. Sobbing. Her entire body was shaking with the force of it.

"Yes. I'm alive, Laura. I'm so sorry I let you down."

"Let me down? You saved us." Her voice was muffled because she had moved to press it back against his chest.

"I didn't save you."

"You did." She looked up then, tears still pouring down her face. "I don't care. I don't even care. All I care about is that you're here. You're alive. Abby is here. She's alive."

"And you're here. Alive." His own voice was shaky. It had been very, very close. Those statements were not a given. They could have easily all three been dead.

"Yes. We're alive!" Laura's sobs were now a laugh. A celebration of triumph.

Laura's smile fell away. "Did they catch him? Mahoney? Did they catch him?"

"Mahoney? Is that the man in the suit?"

Laura nodded.

"Yeah. They caught him. He is out front, in handcuffs, right now."

More tears. So many. Too many. "He killed Josh, Seth. It wasn't some random mugging. He told me. He killed Josh on purpose."

"What? Why? Did he tell you why?"

Laura pulled away then and Seth felt the cold even though he still had a very clingy Abby in his lap. "Yeah. Mahoney is some drug king. Josh found evidence about him, and Mahoney wants that evidence."

"That's what was in the box?"

"Yeah, he realized what Mahoney was, so he gathered some documents that will incriminate Mahoney. That's what this whole thing has been about. Josh wasn't a criminal."

Seth reached out and took Laura's hand. It wasn't as good as hugging her, but he would take contact with this woman any way he could get it. "You were right, Laura. Josh was a good and honorable man. Your husband was a hero."

Laura squeezed his hand. "Thank you. I'm so glad."

Seth saw the lead officer standing in the cabin's doorway. He didn't know how long the man had been there, or how much he had overheard, but Seth appreciated him waiting. At Seth's look, the man walked in. "Laura, this is Lieutenant McCoy, the head of the local SWAT team. He's the one who rescued you."

Laura let go of his hand and stood up. Seth also managed to stand, though it was made more difficult by Abby's body still clinging.

Lieutenant McCoy reached out and shook Laura's hand. "It's real nice to meet you, Mrs. Donovan. And I couldn't have rescued you if Seth here hadn't found us and told us what was happening."

"Well, thank you. Both of you. Thank you very much."

"Ma'am, you and your daughter are okay? Not hurt?"

Laura reached out and rubbed Abby's back. "No. Somehow, we're both okay."

It wasn't just some random somehow, though. It was because God had laid His hand over them and protected them. He had seen them through this storm. And He would see them through the next couple of weeks, too.

Seth intended to mention counseling to Laura. Both she and Abby would probably benefit from talking about everything that happened. Finding a sense of safety again. And him, too. Seth wanted to talk to someone. Clear his head. And make sure he learned all the lessons God had taught him the past few days. The past few years, for that matter.

SIXTEEN

"Seth. Go see Seth." Abby's little voice was insistent, full of energy now that her fever was gone. If this was any indication, Laura was going to have a very strong-willed teenager on her hands in a few years.

"Yes, Abby. We're going to go see Seth." Laura tried to infuse her voice with patience, but she had already said these words at least a dozen times today. And it was still early morning.

"Now." Laura wanted to smile when she saw Abby with her arms crossed and a scowl on her little face. It was a pose that Laura often assumed when she was trying to be stern with Abby.

It seemed that Abby was trying to reverse the process. Yep, Laura was going to be in serious trouble when this little girl got older.

Laura looked at the clock and then stood

from where she had been sitting on a bed in the hotel they had stayed at last night. It was still too early for visiting hours at the hospital, but Abby seemed to be done waiting in the small room. So was Laura, for that matter.

"Okay, baby. Let's go run some errands, and then it will be time to go see Seth."

"Seth." Abby's voice was definitive. A statement of fact. Trouble.

Laura took Abby to a big-box retail store to pick out a gift for Seth. It wasn't ideal, but the store was open and it was large enough to distract Abby until they could go to the hospital. Once there, the girl had stopped demanding to go see Seth every ten minutes. Instead, she wanted to walk up and down every single aisle, determined to find the perfect gift.

Two hours later, Laura was finally driving toward the hospital. Abby was secured in the back in her car seat, a stuffed bear sitting next to her. The bear was every bit as large as Abby. Abby loved him, and Laura found the gift hilariously appropriate. She was as excited as Abby to see Seth's reaction to her gift.

Some of Laura's mirth faded, though, as they parked the car and entered the hospital. The somber lobby and slow elevator ride to

Seth's floor emphasized the events of the past few days. Laura found Seth's room, set down the massive bear and peeked inside, hoping he was awake. Now that they were here, she wasn't sure anything could keep Abby away. And, if she were honest, Laura wanted to see Seth just as badly. She knew, logically, that he was okay. That he was going to be okay.

He had given Abby the hug she requested yesterday. He hadn't wanted to come to the hospital, let alone take an ambulance there, but the police had insisted. So had his boss, who had arrived on the scene sometime during all the chaos. With a sigh, Seth had climbed into the ambulance and gone to the hospital. The police said he would be admitted for the night just as a precaution.

Laura mentally kicked herself when she remembered how she had just stood there yesterday. Her brain unable to comprehend all that had happened.

Her husband's death wasn't an accident. Victor Mahoney had been watching her for months. A criminal had been a part of her every move for months and she hadn't even known. And then, in the course of days, Laura had been shot at, had taken her daughter on the run, had been captured and had thought that she and Abby were going to die. It was too much.

Far too much if she factored Seth into the whole complication. Seth the park ranger. Seth the critic who had judged her father. Seth the hero who had saved them. Seth the man. The man who had awakened feelings in Laura she had thought were gone forever.

With those feelings churning in her stomach, Laura saw Seth sitting in the hospital bed watching television. She knocked lightly on the door that was slightly ajar.

Seth looked over at her and smiled. "Hey. Come in, come in." He turned off the television and set down the remote control. Laura stood there looking at him. She had known he was okay, but a wave of relief hit her when she saw him awake and smiling.

"Seth!" Abby ran over to the bed and held out her arms. Seth was leaning over the bed railing to pick her up when Laura realized what he was about to do.

"Seth, wait. Don't pick her up." He already had Abby sitting in his lap by the time Laura made it to the bed. "Seth, you shouldn't have done that. You could have hurt yourself."

"I'm fine, Laura. This whole thing is an overreaction by the doctors. I should get sprung from this place today." Seth turned and winked at Abby, who promptly tried to jump off his lap. Seth wrapped his arms around her. "Whoa there, Abby McDabby. Where're you going?"

"Present, Mama!"

Seth was looking at Abby and Laura with a smiling question on his face.

"Abby picked out a present for you."

Abby nodded and then reached up to cover Seth's eyes. "No peeking."

Laura could see that Seth had obliged Abby and closed his eyes. She retrieved the bear from the hallway, and brought him into the room. When she was holding the bear in front of Seth's face, Abby moved her hands and spoke. "Okay, Seth. Look."

Seth opened his eyes and took in the giant Smokey Bear. His eyes traveled from the tan hat to the plastic shovel the bear was holding to the blue pants. Laura saw him bite his lip. Hopefully, he thought it was as funny as Laura did.

He looked at Laura. "Was this your idea?"

Laura tried to talk through her smile. "Nope. Abby walked up and down every single aisle and picked this out herself."

Abby looked proud. "It's a bear."

"Yep, it's a great bear, Abby. Thank you."

"Welcome." With that, Abby turned to snuggle into Seth's chest.

Still grinning like a loon, Laura set the bear down on one of the chairs in the room. She sat in another chair.

"So, you're really going home today?"

Seth nodded. "I should be released this afternoon." He looked at Abby. "She's asleep."

"She didn't sleep very much last night. By the time we spoke with the police, it was pretty late. Then she was excited about being in a hotel room."

Seth's voice was all tease. "I bet. She was probably awed by the electricity and running water."

Laura felt herself blush. "Very funny, Mr. Park Ranger." He looked pleased with himself.

"Were you all able to sleep in this morning at least?"

Laura snorted. "Hardly. Abby woke up at the crack of dawn, all eager to see you." She leaned forward in the chair to brush a piece of hair out of Abby's eyes. "You're fortunate the hospital has set visiting hours, or else she would have been here to see you before the sun rose."

Seth reached out and took hold of Laura's hand. "I wouldn't have minded." He looked at her for a long moment before speaking in that same serious tone. "I was worried about both of you. I missed you."

Seth couldn't have kept the admission inside. It was the truth. He had been missing them—ever since he had stepped inside that ambulance. Once the initial rush of being admitted to the hospital was over, he'd been able to sit and think. About his past. About his future.

Laura pulled her hand from his. She put her hands beside her, gripping the edge of the chair so that Seth could see the color of her skin change where the pressure was the greatest. She looked scared, and it made a lump of fear and panic rise up in his throat.

"Laura—"

"I'm sorry." She blurted it out before he could finish his question.

"Sorry? What in the world are you sorry for?" Seth couldn't think of a single thing she needed to apologize for.

Laura had tears in her eyes. "I'm so sorry for everything. This is all my fault."

Seth opened his mouth to reassure her, but

she held up one of her hands. "Wait. Let me say this. Please." Seth closed his mouth and nodded.

"Thank you. I know you're going to disagree with me, but I'm right. Victor Mahoney came here because of me. You spent all those hours being hunted in the woods because of me. You got *shot* because of me." Her voice cracked on the word *shot*, and it broke Seth's heart. She took a shaky breath and continued. "I have brought nothing but trouble and turmoil into your life. I'm so sorry." Laura looked down at her lap, not meeting Seth's gaze.

"I'm not." He said it quietly. With as much certainty and conviction as he could possibly put into two little words. Laura lifted her head and looked at him, but he couldn't read her face. Seth knew without being told that this was one of those life-altering moments. *Give me the words, God. Please, let her understand.* "I'm grateful." He ignored Laura's skeptical face and continued. "I've spent most of the morning thanking God for what He did."

Laura's face was still blank. Unreadable. So was her voice. "What He did." She made it a statement, not a question.

"Yes. What He did."

Laura looked at Seth then, met his gaze and held it for several long seconds. "What did He do, Seth?" Her voice was a whisper, full of emotion.

"He led me to you." With a smile to the little girl sleeping against him, he added, "And Abby."

Laura just watched him. Seth hoped she was listening with an open heart. "I was so alone before I met you, Laura. I know you think that you were the recluse. The only one hiding. But that's not true."

Slow tears began to roll down Laura's precious face. Seth reached out and wiped them away with his fingers, loving the feel of her skin.

"I've been hiding. From my family. From God. From my future."

More slow tears.

"You changed all that. You woke me up." He smiled. "You and this wonderful little girl made me realize what I can have." Seth swallowed. "And I want it."

Laura's eyes widened slightly. She covered her mouth with one hand, as though to hold in more tears. Seth hoped they weren't the sad kind.

"I want it with you, Laura. It's been crazy and incredibly fast, but I have fallen in love with you. And I don't want to let you go."

A sob escaped from behind Laura's hand, and Seth felt like his heart would break. He couldn't tell if she was upset or overwhelmed.

"I need to go home. Back to my family."

She nodded and looked down at her lap again. Seth cringed as he realized he was bungling this. He grabbed her hand and held tight, determined to get it all out as quickly as possible. "But I'm coming back. For you. To you."

Laura looked at him, blinking the tears from her eyes. "What?"

"I meant it when I said that you're it for me. And I want to be it for you. That means I need to step up and become the kind of man who could possibly be worthy of you and Abby."

"Worthy? Seth, you don't have to prove anything to me."

Seth smiled. "Maybe not. But I need to prove something to myself. I want to be proud of who I am. I need to go back to my family and make amends. I need to tell them that I'm sorry I rejected them, ran from them. I need to try to repair our relationship." His smile grew. "And I need to tell them about you and Abby."

Seth sat up as straight as he could while in a hospital bed with a toddler on his lap. "And then, Laura Donovan, I'm coming back here. I plan to court you. To show you that I would make a good husband to you and a good father to Abby. I'll wait as long as it takes to make you both mine."

Laura stood and walked toward the windows. Seth wished he could see her face. At least then he would feel like he had a shot at guessing what she was feeling. Was she happy? Was she trying to find a way to let him down easy? Seth was pretty sure she was scared. He could deal with her fears. With enough time and patience, she would realize what he already knew—they were perfect together. They weren't perfect people, but they could create something wonderful together.

"I won't be here."

Laura's voice was quiet, but Seth heard her. "What?"

"I'm leaving." She was still looking out that blasted window.

"Okay, where are we going?"

Laura did turn then. "We?"

Seth tried to impart every bit of his intention and will into his words. "Yes, we. I meant what I said, Laura. Unless you flat out reject me, I intend to pursue you romantically. I can't do that if we're living in two different places."

Laura just looked at him like he was nuts. Seth felt a little crazy, to be honest. But he was meant to be with this woman. So he would put his trust and his faith in God and accept whatever this relationship brought his way.

"I—I don't know where. I just know I need to go somewhere new. I was hiding. I went out into the world and it hurt me. So I ran home, to a place where there were no people to break my heart."

Seth tried to be patient and let her finish.

"But that's not living. Life is scary and hard. And wonderful. My dad never wanted me to stay on the mountain. He pushed me to go to college. He encouraged me to date. To experience the world. And I did. I met a wonderful man and we created an incredible daughter."

Looking at Abby, Seth had to agree.

"And Josh wouldn't want me to close myself off from the world. He would want me to be happy. For Abby to have the fullest life possible." Laura looked upward and snorted. "I bet they have both been watching me from heaven. Probably yelling at me. Telling me to get up and go find happiness."

She looked back at Seth, meeting his gaze directly. "I'm ready to do that. I'm going to find a nice place and I'm going to live there. *Live.*" Laura's face looked intense, a fire in her eyes. "You said that you will go wherever I am. Me, too. I need you to know I would do the same for you."

Her, too?

Laura moved to stand directly in front of Seth. She still looked determined, but also vulnerable. "I want to go somewhere and live again. With you."

Seth felt all the tension leave his muscles. He reached out and held her face, palms of his hands resting on her cheeks.

He wanted to let her finish.

He wanted to kiss her.

"Abby and I want to be with you."

Seth leaned forward and gently pressed his lips against hers. "I love you, Laura. I want to go slow. I want to be careful with you. But I don't need time to know that I love you. And Abby."

Laura's smile wasn't the least bit vulnerable now. "I love you, too, Seth. We both do."

Seth didn't need anyone to point out God's hand in this development. He sent up a burst of gratitude. He dropped his hands from her face, moving them to hold hers between their bodies. "You know, I'm from a place in Oregon called Carter City. It's a small town, but the people are wonderful. All in all, it's not a bad place to live."

Laura smiled her beautiful smile again, squeezing both of her hands. "Really, now? Tell me more."

EPILOGUE

Two Years Later

Laura sat in the passenger side of the Jeep thinking about circles. Circles and cycles and circumstances that seemed random but had to have been preordained.

"What are you thinking about so hard, pretty girl?"

Seth's voice was teasing and warm and happy. Laura loved that he sounded so incredibly joyful. He reached out and held Laura's hand, keeping his other on the steering wheel of the SUV he was driving. He ran his thumb over a wedding ring. Her wedding ring. The one he had placed on her finger two days ago.

"I was thinking about the first time you drove up this mountain."

Seth squeezed her hand. "If I ever needed

proof that God exists, I have it. He surely sent me to find you."

Laura snorted. He could be such a sap at times.

"That's one way to look at it, I suppose. The other way would be that you drove up a mountain, found a crazy recluse and almost died." She was teasing. Mostly. Though she had found peace and happiness since their ordeal on the mountain, she would never be able to entirely joke about the terror of those days.

"Laura." Seth's voice was loving and almost chiding. "I drove up a mountain alone and ashamed and came back down complete and free."

Laura was silent for a moment. "You know, for a park ranger, you sure can say the sweetest things."

"They're true." He looked at her face briefly, then returned his gaze to the road. "I miss Abby. Maybe we should have brought her with us."

Laura laughed. She couldn't help herself. Abby had Seth wrapped around her little kindergartner finger. Like Laura, Abby had been blessed with a biological father who loved her. Like Laura, Abby had lost that biological father. And, like Laura, God had sent Abby a man—a new father—one who would love her with every bit of his being. Laura frequently gave Seth a hard time about his mushiness where Abby was concerned, but he would just smile and shrug his shoulders.

Of course, Seth wasn't the only one. Abby was staying with Seth's parents while he and Laura had their honeymoon at the cabin. They spoiled Abby about as much as Seth did. Actually, all of Seth's family spoiled Abby. And Laura. From the second Laura and Abby had come to Carter City, they had been surrounded by grandparents and parents and brothers and sisters and cousins and nieces and nephews. It was unfamiliar and overwhelming and often exhausting. It was also wonderful. Laura delighted in the fact that Abby was growing up in the middle of such a large, loving family.

The terrain got slightly rougher and Seth let go of Laura's hand so he could use both hands to drive. "Hey," he said with a grin, "you wanna reenact our first meeting?"

Laura crossed her arms in mock irritation. "Very funny, *Ranger.*" She rolled her eyes at his satisfied smile. Feeling like her heart was almost too full of joy, Laura closed her eyes and said a prayer that had almost become instinctual.

Oh, God, I can't believe You gave us this man. Thank You.

* * * * *

*If you liked this story, pick up this
Love Inspired Historical book
from Victoria Austin:*

Family of Convenience

*Find more great reads at
www.LoveInspired.com*

Dear Reader,

Thank you so much for reading Seth and Laura's story. This is my first book for Love Inspired Suspense. I'm a big fan of stories involving suspense, love and faith and am delighted to share this one with you.

Rocky Mountain Showdown is about trying to be safe in a dangerous world. It's also about dealing with shame. My guiding Bible verse for this book was Isaiah 54:4. It talks about forgetting the shame of our youth. I love that thought—that today's trials will become not just something of the past, but something in the past that we are able to forget.

This world is scary and hard and uncontrollable. Though I try not to, I mess up on a daily basis. I'm familiar with shame and regret and despair. But I'm also familiar with hope. With Jesus and His promise. It's my sincere wish that you know Him, too.

I would love to hear from you. You can find my email address and social media links on my website at www.victoriawaustin.com.

Victoria Austin

Get 4 FREE REWARDS!

We'll send you 2 FREE Books plus 2 FREE Mystery Gifts.

Love Inspired* books feature contemporary inspirational romances with Christian characters facing the challenges of life and love.

FREE
Value Over
$20

MUST ♥ DOGS COLLECTION

SAVE 30% AND GET A FREE GIFT!

Finding true love can be "ruff"— but not when adorable dogs help to play matchmaker in these inspiring romantic "tails."

YES! Please send me the first shipment of four books from the **Must ♥ Dogs Collection**. If I don't cancel, I will continue to receive four books a month for two additional months, and I will be billed at the same discount price of $18.20 U.S./$20.30 CAN., plus $1.99 for shipping and handling.* That's a 30% discount off the cover prices! Plus, I'll receive a FREE adorable, hand-painted dog figurine in every shipment (approx. retail value of $4.99)! I am under no obligation to purchase anything and I may cancel at any time by marking "cancel" on the shipping statement and returning the shipment. I may keep the FREE books no matter what I decide.

☐ 256 HCN 4331   ☐ 456 HCN 4331

Name (please print)

Address   Apt. #

City   State/Province   Zip/Postal Code

Mail to the **Reader Service:**
IN U.S.A.: P.O. Box 1867, Buffalo, NY. 14240-1867
IN CANADA: P.O. Box 609, Fort Erie, Ontario L2A 5X3

NEW ENGLAND

From the majestic mountains to the glorious seashore, experience the beauty New England offers the romantic heart. Four respected authors will take you on an unforgettable trip with true-to-life characters.

Here's your ticket for a refreshing escape to the Northeast. Enjoy the view as God works His will in the lives of those who put their trust in Him.

paperback, 476 pages, 5 ³⁄₁₆" x 8"

♥ ♥ ♥ ♥ ♥ ♥ ♥ ♥ ♥ ♥ ♥ ❤ ♥ ♥ ♥ ♥ ♥ ♥ ♥ ♥ ♥

Please send me _____ copies of *New England*. I am enclosing $5.97 for each. (Please add $2.00 to cover postage and handling per order. OH add 6% tax.)

Send check or money order, no cash or C.O.D.s please.

Name_____

Address _____

City, State, Zip _____

To place a credit card order, call 1-800-847-8270.
Send to: Heartsong Presents Reader Service, PO Box 721, Uhrichsville, OH 44683
♥ ♥ ♥ ♥ ♥ ♥ ♥ ♥ ♥ ♥ ❤ ♥ ♥ ♥ ♥ ♥ ♥ ♥ ♥

Hearts♥ng Presents
Love Stories Are Rated G!

That's for godly, gratifying, and of course, great! If you love a thrilling love story but don't appreciate the sordidness of some popular paperback romances, **Heartsong Presents** is for you. In fact, **Heartsong Presents** is the *only inspirational romance book club* featuring love stories where Christian faith is the primary ingredient in a marriage relationship.

Sign up today to receive your first set of four never-before-published Christian romances. Send no money now; you will receive a bill with the first shipment. You may cancel at any time without obligation, and if you aren't completely satisfied with any selection, you may return the books for an immediate refund!

Imagine. . .four new romances every four weeks—two historical, two contemporary—with men and women like you who long to meet the one God has chosen as the love of their lives. . .all for the low price of $9.97 postpaid.

To join, simply complete the coupon below and mail to the address provided. **Heartsong Presents** romances are rated G for another reason: They'll arrive *Godspeed!*